# Stone Cold

Between a Stone and a

Hard Place

By Jerry Bader

MRPwebmedia.com/books

Amazon.com/author/jerrybader

# Stone Cold

## Between A Stone and a Hard Place

Written by Jerry Bader

Illustrations by Paola Ceccantoni



ISBN Paperback: 978-1-988647-52-4

Hard Cover: 978-1-988647-53-1

Ebook: 978-1-988647-54-8

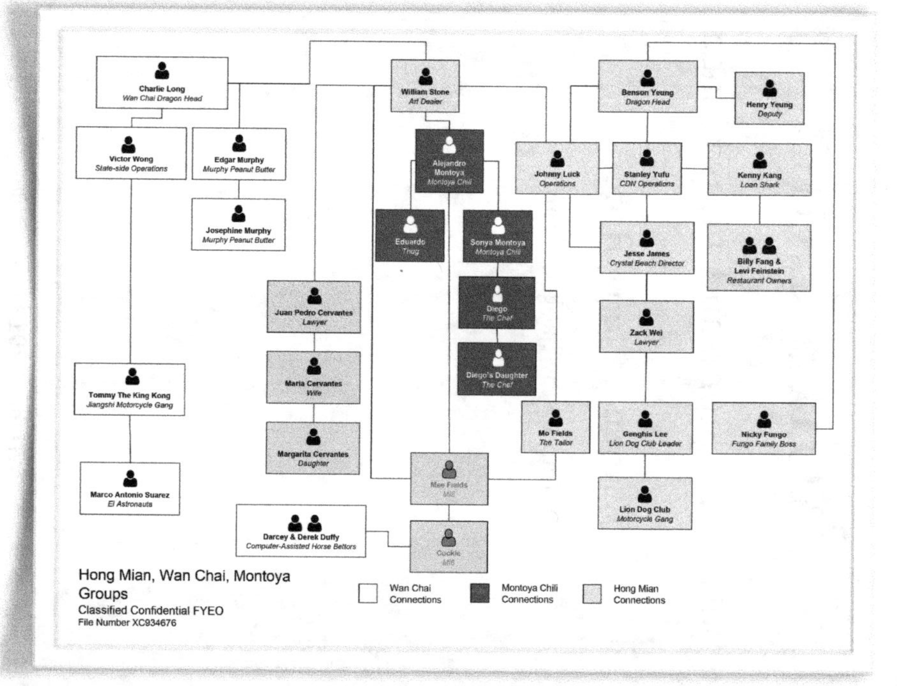


**Hong Mian, Wan Chai, and
Montoya Crime Families
Classified Confidential**

For Your Eyes Only

**Incident At La Galeria de Rosa**

# 1
## Incident At La Galeria de Rosa

**Present Day**

Margarita Cervantes is in love, or least she thinks she is. At eighteen years of age her curiosity, hormones, and fascination with a handsome Englishman has coalesced into what one might call love, or at least infatuation. Margarita is the daughter of Juan Pedro Cervantes; a lawyer who handles the legal needs of William Stone, a retired English military man with more than a shadowy past, and an even darker, more sinister present. Stone runs *La Galeria de Rosa*, The Pink Gallery, in Soho, Palermo, Argentina. He is also a very rich man having inherited one point seven billion dollars in Murphy Peanut Butter Company stock, plus homes in Kentucky, California, and France, all from his former widowed employer.

It's not Stone's wealth that attracts the teenager but rather the visceral air of danger and intrigue that surrounds him. In Margarita's case this aura of danger is not imagined, as she has witnessed it firsthand. She knows her situation is near-hopeless as Stone's heart belongs to a pretty blonde ex jockey that runs a racetrack and gambling operation in Los Angeles for the most powerful triad in the United States, the Hong Mian. But we are getting ahead of ourselves; first there is the problem of the black limousine that just pulled up in front of the pink-painted art gallery that now serves as Stone's offshore hideaway. Margarita enters Stone's office in the back of the gallery, "I see you took down the Botero."

Stone points to a large tube in the corner of the room, "I'm sending it to the States."

Margarita knows exactly what that means. He's sending it to the pretty blonde American. "You're sending it to Jesse?" Stone doesn't answer. She continues, "I think we have a customer. A black limo just pulled up in front."

Stone gets up from behind his desk and picks up the tube and hands it to Margarita, "We're running an art gallery not a bodega… they have customers, we have clients. Take this to the FedEx depot down the street. I'll look after the client."

Margarita gives him a look. "Is that what we're doing? Running an art gallery?" She doesn't wait for a reply. She knows he won't rise to the bait. She thinks, 'one day he'll understand my value. One day he'll let me in on what he's really doing.'

Margarita takes the tube and heads for the front of the gallery. A thirty-five, maybe fifty-year-old Chinese man, it's hard to tell, in the latest European designer threads is carefully examining the series of watercolors that hang on the gallery's walls. Two bulky Chinese bodyguards bracket the front door. A driver stands on the curb outside scanning the street while smoking a foul smelling Chinese cigarette. Margarita, notices the bulges in their stylish suit jackets... trouble is coming.

Most young women would be scared, but not Margarita. The smell of danger only serves to get her near-adult engine revving. Perhaps it's the danger that trumps her knowledge that Stone loves someone else; maybe if she acts, it will prove to him that she's a viable alternative to the tough California blonde he obviously misses. As she leaves the gallery for the FedEx depot she thinks, 'this isn't the first time he's needed my help.'

After dropping off the package at the FedEx store she goes to her father's office across the street beside the family townhouse. Her father's secretary is a plump middle-aged woman; she reminds Margarita that today is Wednesday, the day Juan Pedro spends the afternoon at the *Hipodromo Argentino* racetrack.

Margarita calls her mother and tells her to meet her downstairs in front of her father's office. She goes to his desk and retrieves a key to a closet used for supplies. She opens the closet and grabs a .38 caliber revolver, a German Blaser R8 hunting rifle, and a Sako Model 85 Arctos.
As she leaves her father's private office, she hands the Sako to the secretary and orders her to

follow. The bewildered legal secretary does what she's told. The two women exit the law office where Maria Cervantes, Margarita's mother, is waiting. When she sees her teenage daughter and her husband's secretary exit the building heavily armed, she is not shocked. Ever since the Englishman arrived on the scene she's learned to accept the inevitable disquieting situations. Margarita slaps the Blaser into her mother's chest. Her mother has no idea how it works. The three women cross the street like the Earp brothers making their way to the O.K. Corral.

When they arrive at the front door of the pink-painted gallery, their way is blocked by the heavyset driver who is busy watching a Chinese version of Bruce Lee's Kung Fu classic *Enter The Dragon* on his cell phone. He looks up to see the three armed-women standing in front of him. He starts to laugh. Mrs. Cervantes looks down at the Blaser she's holding. She's scared. The Chinese chauffeur continues laughing as he ignores the women and goes back to his movie.

Mrs. Cervantes swings the butt end of the rifle around hitting the driver square in the jaw. He goes down like Smokin' Joe Frazier getting hit with a George Foreman Grill. The two thugs guarding the door turn around to see the three women aiming their weapons directly at their chests with nothing but the plate-glass window between them. They see their colleague unconscious on the ground. They raise their hands. The women enter the gallery.

Margarita: "Watch these two *pendejos* while I check on William. They move… shoot the fuckers."

Margarita's mother looks at her daughter and shakes her head: "I see your English is getting more colorful by the day."

Margarita ignores her mother and walks into Stone's office. Stone is sitting facing the door holding a Glock aimed at the chest of the Chinese gangster. Margarita jams the .38 into the small of the mobster's back.

Stone: "I think we're done here. Best you leave before my assistant get's nervous."

**The Ghost of William Stone**

# 2
## The Ghost of William Stone

**Ten Years Earlier**

William Stone is a ghost: not the spooky white sheet blowing in the midnight air kind of ghost, nor even the chain dragging Marley-style effigy created by Dickens. He is a living, breathing human being, working for a private boutique investment firm in Hong Kong. The problem is Major William Stone, raised in a small orphanage on the outskirts of London, died in the Falkland Conflict in 1982, leaving no family or relatives to mourn his passing. This regrettable history makes Major Stone the perfect vessel for certain clandestine secretive government agencies to use to hide the identity of Jacob Conrad.

Conrad is the military-trained financial wizard that MI6 used to manipulate the London Interbank Offered Rate, known as the Libor, in order to destabilize certain uncooperative financially strapped regimes.

When it came to wheeling and dealing in the financial services industry Conrad was the master. He used his charm, high-end madams, underworld connections, and carefully cultivated relationships with international drug cartels to influence or blackmail enough high-profile traders to establish a rate that served his Vauxhall Cross, Section Six masters.

Unlike his greedy colleagues who were in it to make a shit-pile of dough, he saw himself as a patriot working for Queen and country. That is until a Canadian Internet news startup with a hard-on for sensational stories started to investigate, resulting in the whole house of cards collapsing. Corruption, money market and interest rate manipulation, and scandal exploded across the front pages of the English tabloids like a bad case of food poisoning.

Careers were at stake, minister-level politicians, government bureaucrats, and of course, those shadowy MI6 fellows that nobody talks about, all ran for cover. Someone was needed to take one for the team, and the patsy status had no other place to land than on the broad shoulders of faithful government servant Jacob Conrad. Someone had to carry the can, and the logical choice was Conrad.

There were those who objected knowing that if Conrad were incarcerated for doing his duty, the next time someone like him was asked to serve, the answer would be a resounding, shove-it where the sun don't shine.

A solution was found. Not a perfect solution, but a solution nonetheless. Conrad was tried in a quick, below the radar London trial where he took complete responsibility for his actions, blaming it on greed, alcohol, and cocaine. The fact that he personally never profited from the financial manipulations, and that he left the lascivious excesses to those he needed to influence, made little difference to the judge, jury, and limited media that were allowed to witness the circus – as usual national security was used as the excuse for the secretive nature of the proceedings. Conrad was convicted and sentenced to fourteen years in prison.

After a time, the public moved on to other scandals leaving Conrad to rot quietly in jail. Eventually a small obituary notice appeared in the back page of the financial section of the *Guardian*: "Financial criminal Jacob Conrad died early this morning in HM Prison Belmarsh by hanging himself with a bed sheet." With Conrad supposedly dead, the path was clear for his ultimate reemergence as Major William Stone. The process was aided by the technical expertise of an MI6 cyber boffin; who with a few judicious clicks of the mouse, resurrects Jacob Conrad as Major William Stone (Retired), complete with a new date-of-birth and revised military service record; and so Jacob Conrad becomes William Stone, a Hong Kong investment dealer and retired expat soldier making his way in the big swinging dick environment of Asian financial chicanery.

**Mr. Long and The Laughing Monkey**

# 3
## Mr. Long and The Laughing Monkey

Lockhart Road in the Wan Chai area of Hong Kong is known for its cacophony of noise, neon, scantily clad women, and the easy availability of drugs. It is a favorite haunt of the young, rich, and foolish expat English stockbrokers that used to be called big swinging dicks when Gordon Gekko was in fashion. Today they're still rich, still swinging, and still dicks. You can chalk the behavior up to the pressure of the job, or just being far away from home with more money than is reasonable, and fewer inhibitions than is necessary. One such palace of neon depravity is The Laughing Monkey, owned by Charlie Long, the upstart Dragon Head of the triad that takes its name from the district. Mr. Long owns many places along the Lockhart strip but The Laughing Monkey is the biggest, brightest, and probably the safest place on the strip since it serves as Mr. Long's headquarters.

Tonight William Stone is there with the CEO and President of a Toledo grocery store chain looking for the capital needed for an aggressive expansion initiative. Stone sits in the middle of a large semicircular black leather settee nursing a watered-down Vodka Collins. In front of him is a round glass table littered with empty bottles of expensive Scotch and well-used glasses. On one side is the grocery CEO who snorts cocaine off the breasts of a twenty-year-old Chinese beauty while on the other side the President of the company massages the inner thigh of what could be the cocaine girl's twin sister.

Mr. Long approaches, "Good evening, Mr. Stone." He ignores the two preoccupied Americans. "Or should I call you Major?" Stone starts to rise but Long waves a hand signaling him to stay seated. Long turns to his bodyguard, a man whose muscular frame strains the fabric of his tight fitting expensive Italian-cut suit. Long says something in Chinese. The man moves off to watch from the bar, ready to reengage if anyone is stupid enough to move against his boss.

Stone takes a sip of his drink. "Just Stone is fine."

Long waves to one of the hostesses who immediately scurries over to where her boss is standing. The two Americans finally realize Stone is talking to someone and that another beautiful young woman has arrived. Long smiles at the men, "I am your host, Mr. Long, welcome to The Laughing Monkey. I'm afraid I need to talk to your friend Mr. Stone, but Miss Tang will see that your every need is looked after, on the house of course." He nods his head in a mock bow to each of the Americans, "Mr. Stone can you please come with me?"

Stone, Long, and the bodyguard disappear up a flight of stairs to Long's private suite of offices. Long sits behind his desk while the bodyguard stands beside the door. "I noticed you weren't partaking of the entertainment, we can always find you something, or someone, more to your liking."

Stone smiles, acknowledging Long's offer. "That's very kind of you Mr. Long, but this is work. I like my vices as much as the next man, but I take care to separate work from pleasure."

Long: "A wise philosophy Mr. Stone… a very wise philosophy indeed, which is exactly why I want to hire you." He reaches under his desk and retrieves a brown leather attaché case. He places it on the desk within Stone's reach. "Please Mr. Stone, take a look, it's unlocked."

Stone leans forward, undoes the metal clasps, and opens the case. He looks inside. He sees stacks of neatly wrapped hundred dollar US bills. He closes the briefcase and leans back in his chair. "That's a lot of money."

Long: "Fifty thousand dollars to be exact."

Stone: "But I already have a job and it pays substantially more than that."

Long: "Oh, I am aware Mr. Stone, but you misunderstand. All I need is for you to do your job."

Stone: "I'm afraid you'll have to be more explicit."

Long: "Tomorrow, an Edgar T. Murphy and his wife Josephine will be arriving at your office. Mr. Murphy and his wife are majority shareholders of a large peanut butter manufacturing and distribution company in the United States. They specialize in producing house brands for the big supermarket chains. They also import and sell a specialty brand of imported peanut butter chili from Cacaloxuchitl, Mexico and sell it to specialty distributors. Unfortunately the company is going broke. The cost of manufacturing has risen dramatically while competition has driven the wholesale price lower. Profits have disappeared.

Murphy has made some unfortunate personal investments, and he's dipped his hands into the company cookie jar in order to prop up his lifestyle, one that includes his wife's love of expensive thoroughbred racehorses. The stress of the situation has led to an over indulgence in both liquid and powder stress reducers. In short, Edgar and Josephine Murphy are fucked, unless they get an influx of cash. And I would like you to be their guiding angel, delivering exactly what they need to survive, cash.

Stone: "And what do you get out of this deal. You're not in the losing money business."

Long: "Distribution Mr. Stone… distribution. Murphy Peanut Butter has one of the largest fleets of trucks in the United States, and they deliver their product to every state in the Union, across Canada, and into Mexico. All we ask is that they deliver some of our product from our Mexican friends at the same time."

Stone: "And in return you'll bail out the company and replace the embezzled funds?"

Long: "That's correct."

Stone: "And all I have to do is convince them to go along with the deal."

Long pauses for a moment before he speaks. "Not quite Mr. Stone. We need someone we can trust on the ground, someone who can manage the operation, keep the Murphys in line, and make sure the company and the authorities don't get too curious about the various brands of Mexican product being imported and distributed."

Stone: "What makes you think I'm the man for the job?"

Long: "Major Stone… or should I call you Commander Conrad… I am very sure you're exactly the man for the job. You come highly recommended by our mutual friends in Legoland."

Stone smiles at the insider nickname for his former employer: "I'm afraid fifty thousand dollars is not going to cut it."

Long: "Oh that. Let's just say the attaché case is a gift from me to you for listening to this proposition. Take the money. It's yours. If you decide to take me up on this opportunity, bring the Murphys to Happy Hills Racecourse tomorrow evening at eight. I'll reserve a table in the dining room. I am sure it will be worth everyone's time. You might want to bring some of that money. You may find it comes in handy."

**If Horses Could Talk**

# 4
## If Horses Could Talk

If racehorses could talk, they'd have one hell of a story to tell. Racing is gambling and where there's money there's crime. More money passes through the wickets at Happy Hills Racecourse in Hong Kong than any other racetrack in Europe or North America. So corruption is inevitable.

Horse racing has employed some of the most inventive cheating schemes ever devised; electric buzzers called machines, payoffs to jockeys to hold horses, and drugs to either enhance or retard a specific horse's performance. The variety of cheating methods employed by jockeys, veterinarians, trainers, owners, and gamblers would impress even Rube Goldberg; but none were more impressive than the one employed by the Wan Chai at the Happy Hills Racecourse in Hong Kong.

Happy Hills is an unusual turf racecourse with a public infield featuring several soccer fields and picnic areas. The public has access to the infield by way of an underground tunnel that is accessed through an entrance in the basement of the grandstand. Running parallel to the public tunnel is a service tunnel used by maintenance crews to service the grandstand, track, and infield facilities. As it happens, the service contract for the racetrack is held by The Laughing Monkey Entertainment Corporation, whose CEO is Charlie Long; when opportunity knocks someone will always answer.

A wise man, maybe it was an FBI Agent, once said that *if criminals were smart, the jails would be empty, and they're not*. No matter how clever a criminal enterprise is, its success depends on its weakness link, people. People talk. You just can't shut them up.

Payoff a jockey to hold the favorite, and he'll brag about it to his girlfriend; have your jockey use a machine to give your horse a boost, and he'll tell his buddies at the bar; have your vet give your horse an injection of some performance enhancing pharmaceutical, and he'll decide to tell his wife; commit a crime, any crime, and people just got to blab about it all over town. All it takes is one pissed off girlfriend, wife, or colleague, and a whole criminal empire can come crashing down. The answer is don't rely on people. Deal directly with the horses. They don't talk.

The maintenance crew of the Happy Hills Racecourse surreptitiously installed twelve metal tubes in the turf under the starting gate. Each foot long tube is loaded with Azaperone (ACE) sedative darts. The tubes are linked together so they can be individually fired wirelessly by a remote operator.

If Charlie Long and associates want a long shot to win, all they need to do is have their operator fire the tranquilizer darts into the long-shot's main competitors. The darts contain just enough sedative to take the edge off the favorite's competitive instincts, insuring the long-shot will win. Ingenious, even crazy, so crazy the idea actually works.

So you may ask, but even this plan requires people, what if someone talks? And the answer is simple. They turn up floating face down in Victoria Harbour.

**A Sure Thing At Happy Hills**

# 5
## A Sure Thing At Happy Hills

The next day the Murphys show up at Stone's office with a letter of introduction from an English venture capital firm that is a friend of a friend in Section Six. It's clear that his ex-employer needs an arm's length cutout to do the dirty work. Stone finds himself between a rock and a hard place. The situation proves the rule, once you're in, you're in for life.

Stone had no idea what benefit there was to the British government in this whole operation, but in the end he understood there really didn't need to be any great master plan behind the scheme. Perhaps the British mandarins were helping an upstart triad boss because he was related to some high-powered government official or some high-ranking military big shot looking to supplement his retirement income. The reason really didn't matter. He was in whether he liked it or not.

Placing him in a private boutique investment firm in Hong Kong wasn't for his benefit, despite the substantial compensation package; it was for future operational scenarios that required remote plausible deniability. Stone understood if things went sideways, he would have to be eliminated. His old pals who put him in the quod for a year before coming up with the phony suicide plan could not afford to have Jacob Conrad reappear even if it was in the far-flung former colony of Hong Kong. Stone got the feeling he was being setup. He would just have to play things out to see if he was still standing at the end of the day.

Stone tells the Murphys that he has set up a dinner meeting with a potential investor that can solve both their personal and business problems. Stone and the Murphys arrive at the Happy Hills Racecourse where they meet Charlie Long, head of the Wan Chai Social Club and owner of The Laughing Monkey Entertainment Corporation. After some drinks and small talk revolving around the exotic nature of Hong Kong and horse racing, Long suggests that they place some bets.

Long: "Mrs. Murphy, I understand you're a connoisseur of thoroughbreds." Josephine Murphy smiles acknowledging that she knows a thing or two about racing. Long turns to Stone, "Did you bring the suitcase?" Stone nods.

Long: "Good." He turns his attention back to Mrs. Murphy. "Let's try a little experiment. You're not familiar with any of the horses running this evening are you?" Both Murphys shake their heads. "Good. So here's what I want you to do. I want you to pick five random numbers from one to ten." Long reaches into his pocket and hands Mrs. Murphy a piece of paper with The Laughing Monkey logo embossed in gold across the top. "Write your numbers down on this."

The Murphys are a little nervous about this game. They didn't come to Hong Kong to get ripped off by some Chinese gangster involved in some racetrack swindle, they heard stories of what goes on in the Tombstone of the Wild East. The Murphys put their heads together and come up with five random numbers that Mrs. Murphy neatly prints on the piece of paper. Long waves his hand in the air and a beautiful hostess almost magically appears beside the table.

Long turns to Stone, "May I have your briefcase please?" Stone reaches under the table to retrieve the briefcase and hands it to Long who hands it to the young woman. He gives her the paper with the numbers on it. He speaks to her in rapid fire Cantonese. "Mr. Stone's briefcase contains fifty thousand US dollars. We've just wagered ten thousand dollars to win on each of the next five races using your randomly selected numbers."

The Murphys look at each other not sure exactly what has just happened. Have they been duped? It wasn't their money. Has Stone just been screwed? What the hell is going on? Long ignores the confused looks and signals the waiter to come over. He delivers more rapid fire Cantonese to the waiter who arrives back within minutes with coffee and pastries before the Murphys had a chance to recover from the shock of Long's cavalier betting.

Long: "I see you're confused, so let me explain. I am not a gambling man. I only bet on sure things. Mr. Stone has filled me in on your situation and I am very interested in your company. I could be convinced to invest, but like I said, I only bet on sure things. If the horses you've picked all win, you are by my reckoning a sure thing, if your selections don't win, then I'm afraid you're a risky gamble, and I don't gamble."

Mr. Murphy looks at Long, "Are you nuts? What kind of businessman are you?"

Long: "I assure you Mr. Murphy, a very careful one. Why don't we just sit back and watch the races while we eat dessert?"

The Murphys seem totally deflated. They've come all this way on the premise that they could save the business and their personal fortune but instead, end up having dinner with a Chinese nut case. Edgar Murphy downs his whiskey sour in one gulp. "This is ridiculous, you people are crazy. I'm leaving." He turns to his wife, "Come on dear. Let's grab a cab back to the hotel."

Josephine Murphy shakes her head. "I want to stay and see the races." Edgar throws his hands up in the air and stomps out of the dining room. Josephine Murphy, William Stone, and Charlie Long sit quietly waiting for the next race to start. Over the next several hours, five races are run, and each time the horse Josephine Murphy and her husband picked wins. Murphy is giddy.

When the last race is completed the attractive hostess arrives back at the table with Stone's briefcase still filled with his initial fifty thousand dollars. The hostess hands Long an official look-ing piece of paper. Long hands it to Mrs. Murphy. It's in Chinese. All she can make out is a number 527,233. She looks at Long and then at Stone. "Do you know what this is?"

Stone takes the piece of paper and looks it over. "This is your winnings, you won 527, 233 Hong Kong dollars."

Murphy: "How much is that in real money?"

Stone: "About $67,450 US dollars… I'll arrange to have the money sent to your personal account back in the States."

Long: "Tomorrow Mr. Stone will bring you and your husband to my office where we can finalize the arrangement for the refinancing of your company."

Murphy: "But how did you do it? You said you're not a betting man and that you only bet on sure things. I've seen every betting scheme in the business, but never one that involved arranging five random winners in a row with no pre-arrangement. It's impossible."

Long: "Nothing is impossible Josephine, can I call you Josephine?"

*Alea iata est*
**The Die Has Been Cast**

**6**
***Alea iacta est***
**The Die Has Been Cast**

It takes several weeks for preparations to be made. Stone ties up loose ends at the investment firm and arranges for the refinancing of the Murphy Peanut Butter Company. With those details looked after, his next job is to create a logistics department that will take over the transportation of product. The company already has the trucks and the drivers, but can they be trusted to move the illegal product without getting suspicious or calling the authorities? New people will have to be brought in who can handle the more sketchy deliveries.

Meanwhile, Stone is expected to assume his duties as the Murphy's chauffeur, a job that more accurately should be defined as their keeper. If they step out of line for any reason, his mandate from Charlie Long is to eliminate them.

As leverage, Stone is made sole heir to the Murphy estates if both happen to die. The Murphys aren't happy about this last-minute wrinkle, but they put up minimum resistance as they have little choice.

And so it begins...

Stone waits for his flight to Los Angeles in the executive lounge of the Hong Kong International

Airport. An attractive Chinese woman holding a cup of coffee approaches, she's accompanied by a well-dressed man. The woman sits down on one side of Stone and the man sits on the other. There are plenty of other empty seats in the lounge but they choose to surround Stone. The man picks up the Wall Street Journal from an empty seat and starts to read. The woman sips her coffee. Their choice of seats is not by accident. The woman speaks in a refined British accent without turning her head, "Good morning Jacob, how are you this lovely morning?"

Stone can feel the pulse in his neck start to pound; his head begins to ache; he shouldn't have packed the Sumatriptan. It seems, far too many people know who he is. Someone at Six has a big mouth, and it just might get him killed. He turns to look at the woman. "What do you want?"

The woman returns Stone's look, "Oh it's not what I want Jacob, it's what 'C' wants." Stone grimaces at the one-letter moniker reserved for the head of MI6.

Stone: "I don't work for Six anymore, and besides, even if I did, I'd need direct confirmation." The woman opens her Louis Vuitton handbag and pulls out an envelope with an official government seal. She hands it to Stone. He examines it trying to determine if it's real or fake. He's not sure which is worse. In either case, it meant trouble.

He opens the sealed envelope pulls out a piece of letterhead with nondescript block letters embossed across the top 'Section Six.' Underneath is the familiar scrawl of the head of MI6 written in signature green ink and signed with the single letter 'C', a practice that goes back a hundred years to the first head of Section Six, Captain Sir Mansfield Cumming. The note is genuine. He reads silently, '*Do whatever they tell you to do. - C*'

The woman takes the letter and envelope from Stone and places it back in her purse. The man on Stone's other side hands him an airline ticket. Stone looks at it. It's for a direct flight to Mexico City.

Stone: "I already have a ticket to LA." The woman sticks out her hand, "Yes, I know, may I please have it." Stone gives the woman his ticket. She takes the ticket and leaves. Stone turns to the man, "Now what?"

The man picks the Wall Street Journal back up, "Now we wait for our flight." He begins to read.

Stone: "And what do I call you?" The man looks over the newspaper, "Everybody calls me Mo, Mo Fields. The pretty lady that just left is Mee." Stone doesn't bother asking any more questions. He knows better. Everything will be revealed in due course.

**Hola Mexico**

# 7
## Hola México

The flight from Hong Kong to Mexico City is uneventful. Mo Fields doesn't talk much. Anytime Stone asks a question, he is greeted by silence, a curt "you'll see," or a comment about how one of the other passengers is dressed. When they arrive at Mexico City International Airport, they are met by Zack Wei, a lawyer who works for the head of the Hong Mian's Canadian operation run by Stanley Yufu. In his younger days, Wei was the leader of the Lion Dogs Motorcycle Club, the street gang that handles Canadian drug distribution for the Hong Mian. The current leader of the Lion Dogs is Genghis Lee, nicknamed The Khan.

The Hong Mian and the Wan Chai are not exactly enemies, but neither are they friends. The upstart new guy on the block, Charlie Long, has aspirations of taking control of the more powerful Hong Mian run by the respected elder, triad statesman, Benson Yeung. The Hong Mian is more powerful, more sophisticated, and less violent in its dealings. That is not to say they shy away from a bullet in the back of the head of anyone who fails to live-up to their obligations. Try to screw Benson Yeung, and you may get a visit from Mo Fields, The Taylor.

Fields actually is a tailor of considerable reputation in Los Angeles, especially among the movers and shakers of tinsel town, a nice cover for his

Hong Mian button man sideline. His duties on this occasion are to see that no harm comes to William Stone, the man in the center of the whole convoluted multi-layered illegal business arrangement. Historically, various government agencies throughout the West have found it convenient to develop relationships with individuals who can act as liaison with certain powerful underworld elements. During WII the FBI found it expedient to use Meyer Lansky to liaison with Lucky Luciano in order to stop Nazi infiltration on the New York docks.

When Section Six needed better intelligence from underworld Hong Kong sources, they opted to use Agent Mee Fields' Chinese-American-English background as the perfect connection. Mo, her ex-Marine sniper husband, became the conduit for communicating with the Hong Mian. In return, Six turned a blind eye to certain illegal London-based Hong Mian operations.

Mo met his wife in London while he was apprenticing as an assistant tailor at a fashionable bespoke tailor shop that catered to government bureaucrats including a number of high-ranking Section Six big shots. Mee held dual citizenship: her mother was a beautiful Chinese-American fashion model in the seventies and her father was the Section Six mandarin in charge of recruitment. Six always has room for an English-American beauty that is fluent in English, Cantonese, Mandarin, and French, especially if daddy is a Six bigwig.

The nameless, bloodless suits that occupy the walnut-paneled offices of Section Six don't trust Charlie Long. They intend to cover their bets. Long is a wild card, with a penchant for rash behavior and impulsive decisions. Benson Yeung on the other hand is thoughtful and measured. His senior executives, his eldest son Henry, Johnny Luck, and Stanley Yufu are also more deliberate and discreet in their dealings, both legal and illegal.

No matter how the game plays out, Six is determined to be on the winning side, and that meant betting on both the Wan Chai and the Hong Mian. The plan is for Stone to employ the Lion Dogs as the drivers, distributors, and collectors for the product that is neither peanut butter nor chili. That meant the Hong Mian would in effect be controlling the distribution of Wan Chai product as well as their own. As long as everyone kept their mouths shut there was no reason the scheme wouldn't work.

The meeting with Alejandro Montoya, the cartel leader, is key to the success of the whole operation. If the Mexican drug czar is uncomfortable dealing with two rival Chinese triads, the whole operation goes up in smoke.  He had to be convinced the plan was the best way to distribute the most cocaine.

Charlie Long was the untested newcomer while Benson Yeung was the stable business alternative. Someday the Wan Chai might supplant the Hong Mian, but that day wasn't coming any time soon, and it may never come. The Hong Mian is a reliable partner that could increase sales and broaden distribution. The plan looked like a winner on paper. Zack Wei explained all the details to Stone during the two and half hour drive from Mexico City to Cacaloxuchitl, where Stone, Wei, and Fields were to meet with Alejandro Montoya, head of the Cacaloxuchitl Cartel.

Alejandro Montoya

# 8
## Alejandro Montoya

Alejandro Ricardo Montoya is the rugged sixty-year-old leader of the Cacaloxuchitl Cartel. The grey-haired patron of the small Puebla town dresses in jeans, work-shirt, and white Stetson cowboy hat. Despite his enormous wealth and power, he cultivates the persona of a man of the people. He knows almost every resident in Cacaloxuchitl by name, most of whom work in his factory or in one of the town's few businesses that are either owned by his daughter, Sonya, or are rented to a property owned by the Montoya Mantequilla de Mani Chili Company. The town is known for its famous peanut butter chili, one of Montoya's semi-legitimate business enterprises, an operation that serves as a mechanism for laundering drug money. The chili company is run by Montoya's daughter, Sonya, who handles the day-to-day chili business, leaving her father free to develop the more profitable cartel business.

Until recently cocaine was smuggled into the States by US-based Mexican gangs. The once reliable Mexican street gangs became major targets of the DEA, putting a significant dent in the movement of product across the border. Customers were getting antsy and Montoya was developing a reputation for unreliability. Competitors were moving in to fill the void, but they too had the same delivery problems.

When Charlie Long came to Montoya with the Murphy Peanut Butter plan, it seemed like all the stars were aligning, except for the fact that Benson Yeung's LA-based Hong Mian and their Buffalo-based Fungo Family partners were Montoya's main US and Canadian distributors.

Charlie Long's operation would be restricted to the smaller less populated markets. The border problem seemed to be solved when Section Six Agent, Mee Fields, paid Montoya a visit, suggesting distribution be managed by the Six-friendly Hong Mian, whose members could be employed by Murphy to deliver the more sensitive product. Charlie Long would assume distribution was being handled by existing Murphy logistic personnel.

Benson Yeung knew the volatile Charlie Long would eventually try to infringe on Hong Mian territory, but controlling the flow of product meant he could cut off Wan Chai's supply anytime he wanted. Success depended on reliable delivery as well as keeping Charlie Long in the dark about the Hong Mian's involvement.

Stone and company arrive in Cacaloxuchitl, a town with just over three thousand residents, about midafternoon. They stop at a dusty roadside café called *Palacio Del Pollo De Diego,* Diego's Chicken Palace. Fields gets out of the car, stretches, and shoos away a number of Diego's future blue-plate specials. He enters the less than palatial chicken joint. The place looks like a semi-demolished relic from the 1950s. What isn't faded or dusty is broken.  A twelve-year-old girl stands behind what is supposed to be a counter: two salvaged whiskey barrels with a slab of wood across the top. The girl turns towards the kitchen and calls for her father, "*Papá viene, es un gringo.*" A weathered unshaven man in his thirties, wearing a denim work shirt and jeans under a filthy apron comes out from the back, "*¿Si, como puedo ayudarle?*"

Fields: "*Buscamos el lugar Montoya.*" The man says something to the little girl who takes Fields by the hand and walks him outside. She points to a dusty unpaved road that leads out of town. "*Continúe así por un kilómetro.*" Fields thanks the little girl. He reaches into his pocket and pulls out a twenty-dollar bill. He hands it to the young girl. She takes the money and runs back into what passes for Cacaloxuchitl's favorite fast-food restaurant.

Fields drives a kilometer down the unpaved road that leads to the Montoya Mantequilla de Mani Chili Company on the outskirts of town. The company compound is gated with barbed wire and multiple cameras facing in each and every direction. Two heavily armed men guard the front gate while others patrol the perimeter. As they approach the front gate Stone notes the heavy security, "That's a hell of a lot of security for a chili manufacturer."

Fields: "But not for a cocaine distributor."

The compound consists of several nondescript buildings as well as a beautiful well-appointed cream-colored adobe hacienda with a terracotta tile roof. It is also heavily guarded. They are ushered into a courtyard surrounded by a patio shielded from the sun by a matching tiled roof. *Señor* Montoya and his daughter Sonya sit drinking Sangria.

Montoya stands to greet his guests, *"Buenas tardes caballeross, y bienvenidos a mi casa."* The men all shake hands and are introduced to Montoya's daughter. Sonya offers the men some cool refreshing Sangria, a welcome regenerative after their long, hot, dusty ride. Once the small talk is out of the way they get down to business.

Montoya explains that the DEA is cracking down on shipments. They've found and destroyed a number of underground tunnels that the Mexican-American street gangs were using to get the drugs across the border. The question became how could the Murphy trucks get the merchandise into the USA without being detected. Stone proposes the solution.

Stone: "Sometimes the simplest solution is the best. The Montoya Mantequilla de Mani Chili Company needs peanut butter to make its chili. Murphy Peanut Butter becomes your exclusive supplier. Every week we send a convoy of trucks loaded with peanut butter to your factory. Murphy Peanut Butter then becomes your exclusive US distributor of chili, so instead of the trucks returning to the US empty, they return with product, half of which is chili and the other half cocaine.

The cocaine can be packaged in similar containers labeled the same as the rest of the real chili, or it can be distinguished with low sodium or diet labels, whatever works better. It can even be packaged in the same containers as the chili in order to help mask the smell from the sniffer dogs. But we don't start shipping powder right away; we just transport peanut butter and chili back and forth across the border until the border guards get used to seeing the Murphy trucks. Eventually, it all becomes boring, mundane routine.

For the first little while they'll check carefully and find nothing illegal; after a while they'll start to slack off; it's human nature. That's when you start sending the cocaine. Occam's Razor, the simplest solution is the best."

Montoya thinks for a moment; he is about to speak when Sonya interrupts: "I like the basic concept, but how do we get our money?"

Montoya reacts with one sweeping motion slapping his forty-year-old daughter across the face almost knocking her out of her chair. Stone starts to rise, but Fields grabs his arm signaling him to mind his own business. Sonya is embarrassed but doesn't say a word.

Montoya: "Sometimes children don't know their place, but she has a point. They'll be a lot of cash that needs to come back across the border."

Stone is angered by Montoya's treatment of his daughter. His violent reaction to her participating in the conversation was uncalled for, but it made clear the kind of man they were dealing with, and perhaps that was the point.

Stone: "Since Murphy Peanut Butter is a customer, you can bill us an inflated price for the product. That way a good deal of the cash will come back to you clean. The excess cash can come back hidden in the shipments of peanut butter."

Sonya stays quiet until all the real business is completed. When the meeting starts to wind down Sonya suggests the men stay overnight and return to the US in the morning. Sonya takes the men on a tour of the chili manufacturing operation, and offers to show them the cocaine building, but Stone declines. Just walking through the building might result in some residue finding its way onto their shoes and that just might alert a sniffer dog at the border.

**Stress Is A Killer**

# 9
## Stress Is a Killer

On the books, William Stone is merely the Murphy's chauffeur, private secretary, and personal assistant. In fact, Stone is supervising the importation of Colombian cocaine from Mexico and distributing it throughout North America by two rival Chinese triads. Each week a fleet of trucks delivers Murphy peanut butter to the Montoya Mantequilla de Mani Chili Company in Cacaloxuchitl, Mexico. Instead of the vehicles returning to the US empty, they are loaded with Montoya Special Brand Chili, half of which is chili and the other half cocaine.

On the surface everyone should be happy, but of course they're not. Mix the Wan Chai, the Hong Mian, Montoya Chili, and Murphy Peanut Butter; add a dash of Section Six and a whole-lot of cash and cocaine, and you've got a recipe for disaster. It's not a question of if, but when, the pot will boil over. Charlie Long doesn't trust Montoya; Montoya is nervous about using the Hong Mian to distribute Long's cocaine; and Benson Yeung is anxious about Long's increasingly frequent intrusions into his territory. Stone just minds his own business and does his job managing the back-and-forth flow of product and cash.

Things start off well enough. Under Stone's attentive eye and financial expertise, the operation works like a dream. The Murphy's personal financial crisis is averted and the value of their stock soars. Despite the return to obscene wealth, the Murphys feel the strain of having William Stone involved in every aspect of their lives. It starts to have an effect.

Edgar Murphy finds solace in the company of Jack Daniels while Josephine Murphy finds comfort by burying her nose in copious piles of Montoya Special Brand Chili. While Josephine manages to retain a semblance of normalcy as a functioning drug addict, her husband becomes a nervous breakdown in waiting. Edgar Murphy falls deeper into the clutches of Gentlemen Jack's fine Tennessee Whiskey while his wife fills her days buying ever more expensive racehorses while consuming an endless supply of readily available cocaine.

Edgar Murphy soon realizes his usefulness as company CEO is all but ceremonial. It's the English chauffeur and minder with the stock manipulation background that's put Murphy's company and personal wealth back on the right side of the ledger. But everything has a price; within two years Edgar Murphy is dead, found on the floor of his office surrounded by a puddle of two hundred and seventy dollar Jack Daniels Number 27.

Several more years go by with things operating smoothly. Everybody is prospering from the unique combination of partners, some more than others. The Hong Mian is raking in the giant

share of white powder profits while the Wan
Chai is left with the scraps, as Charlie Long de-
scribes them, but even the leftovers are substantial enough to boost the financial fortunes of Wan
Chai. The fact is, the Montoya alliance has provided the means for the Wan Chai to become the
second most powerful triad in the United States,
but Charlie Long is determined to be number
one, even if it kills him, and if he doesn't play his
cards right, it will.

As time passes, Long's irritation increases. He
can't crack the Hong Mian's stranglehold on major markets. The combination of the West Coast
Hong Mian and the East Coast Fungo Family appears to be unbreakable.  Instead of being satis-
fied with the new revenue stream, Long gets angry.

It doesn't take a major investigation to find out
there's a hell-of-a-lot of Montoya Special Brand
Chili floating around; product that his people
deny selling. Somebody is double-dealing and
whoever it is must pay. His people just don't have
the wherewithal to pull this off; that rules out a
slow moving Wan Chai Coup. The obvious trai-
tors are Montoya or Section Six, and Long's money is on the arrogant ex colonial assholes that
think they run the world.

With the death of her husband, Josephine Murphy plunges headlong into her two favorite hob-
bies, racehorses and Special Brand Montoya

Chili. Over the years, her behavior becomes ever more erratic. Addicts, no matter how rich, are like unexploded mines just waiting for someone to step on them, and when they do… boom, everything goes to hell in a handbasket.

Long demands action, someone has to pay for his displeasure, unfortunately for Josephine Murphy, his attention falls on her, the weakest link. Murphy is merely a minor irritant, a surplus piece of flotsam and jetsam leftover from the original deal. Despite her irrelevant presence, she has become the initial focus of Long's frustration. She has to go. Long orders Stone to have her killed, and he doesn't care how, as long as it appears to be an accident, and doesn't come back to bit Charlie Long in the ass.

Stone has no choice to follow through on Long's order to eliminate Mrs. Murphy. And so Mrs. Josephine Murphy dies in a car accident in the mountains of Sicily while on a trip to Monreale in order to renegotiate a deal involving the sale of a problem racehorse. This creates a problem for Stone who now inherits one point seven billion dollars of Murphy assets.

The inheritance focuses the tabloid media's dissipated glare on the handsome foreign chauffeur who pockets his boss's fortune. But Stone pulls a mini Howard Hughes, without the crazy, and disappears into semi retirement.

He installs Zak Wei, the Canadian lawyer with the Lion Dog Motorcycle Club ties as CEO. Wei runs the day-to-day operations, both legal and illegal, with Lion Dogs' leader, Genghis The Khan Lee, in charge of distribution. With the company securely in Hong Mian hands, Stone is free to concentrate on making sure the funds keep flowing in the right directions, an assignment that can be accomplished with a computer and a secure Internet connection anywhere in the world.

As soon as the dust settles on Mrs. Murphy's estate, Major William Stone disappears, landing in Palermo, Argentina, as owner of a prosperous art gallery. His only regret is leaving the ex jockey and Hancock Racetrack Director, Jesse James, behind. Stone hopes he will eventually make contact with Jesse. The plan quickly takes a turn when Charlie Long and friends walk into *La Galeria de Rosa*.

**Too Many Cooks**

# 10
## Too Many Cooks

**Present Day**

Charlie Long sits in comfort in the back of the air-conditioned black Cadillac limousine parked in front of the *Palacio Del Pollo De Diego*. He leans over the front seat and hands his bodyguard a photograph of Mee Fields. His man knows what to do. He gets out of the car and goes into the fast food chicken joint. Diego's daughter is behind the counter as usual. He hands her the photograph. She looks, figuring the stranger wants her to identify the attractive Chinese-American woman. She certainly recognizes the woman who pays regular visits to the Montoya compound, each time stopping off at the chicken restaurant for an eighteen-peso espresso, and each time leaving a twenty-dollar tip. She shrugs. The Chinese gangster brushes back his suit jacket revealing his black leather shoulder holster, holding a Norinco QSZ-92 semi-automatic. Diego's daughter turns and calls her father, *"Papá, los malos están aquí."*

Diego comes out from the back of the restaurant. He sees the Chinese gangster. He wipes his hands across his dirty apron and tells his daughter to go in the back. The bodyguard shows Diego the photograph of Mee Fields. He knows the woman from her frequent visits and her kindness to his daughter. He shakes his head denying any knowledge of the woman. The Chinese thug reaches across the wooden slab that functions as a counter and grabs Diego by the collar. He pulls out his semi-automatic and gently runs it down the cheek of the chicken chef before he, not so gently, jabs it under his chin. Diego likes the woman, but he has no intention of dying for her. He nods his head as best he can under the circumstances. He points in the direction of the Montoya compound, "*Montoya… Ella viene a ver a monsieur Montoya.*" The gangster doesn't speak Spanish, but he gets the message.

Charlie Long sits relaxing, drinking Sangria in the patio courtyard of the Montoya hacienda. His bodyguard stands by the door; arms crossed with a bored look on his face. Alejandro and Sonya Montoya sit opposite Charlie Long discussing the success of their co-operative enterprise. So far everything has been cordial, but the conversation is about to take a turn.

Long's eyes keep moving from Montoya to his daughter. She can feel him virtually undressing her with his eyes. She's used to leering men who don't know who she is, but those who do, show respect. Other than this Chinese big shot nobody dares offend Sonya Montoya, nobody that is except her father, whose hair-trigger temper can result in an extra layer of makeup.

Long: "I understand these types of operations have a lot of moving parts, and sometimes the moving parts end up going in different directions."

Alejandro: "I'm not sure what you mean?"

Long chooses his words carefully. He is in Montoya's backyard surrounded by Montoya guns with only a single bodyguard for protection. This is not the time for histrionics or flamboyant demonstrations of muscle; besides, Montoya is the man with the Colombian connection. Without him there is no cocaine, and a move against Montoya would certainly result in Colombian reprisals.

Long: "My people tell me they can't sell any Montoya product to Hong Mian customers, a problem we could chalk up to poor quality, customer loyalty, or fear of retribution. The trouble is, it appears that these potential clients seem to be getting as much Montoya Special Brand Chili as they want, but not from us. And that gives me pause... in fact it makes me very unhappy."

Alejandro: "Charlie, *mi amigo*, you understand we all come to this enterprise with partners, associates, and..." He pauses searching for the right words in English. "Interested parties. Product is being delivered to your customers, you are prospering from the arrangement, and everyone involved is getting... *gordo y feliz.*"

Sonya translates, "Fat and Happy." Her father shoots her a look that silently reminds her to shut up, or pay the consequences.

Long: "You see that's the problem. I'm not happy. Benson Yeung is selling your product making it impossible for me to cut into his market share. It's only a matter of time before he decides to expand into my territory."

Alejandro: "These sales issues are not my problem. I only supply the product. Who you sell to is not my concern."

Long: "Our deal was the Wan Chai would be your exclusive US distributor."

Alejandro: "That was the intent, but unfortunately other concerned parties demanded a more liberal distribution network. Benson Yeung has many friends in high places, and they insisted the Hong Mian be part of the operation. Better to be a small part of something big, rather than a big part of nothing at all."

Long: "And that's why Mee Fields has been paying you regular visits?"

Montoya nods, confirming Long's suspicion.

Long: "You have to make a choice; it's either the Hong Mian or the Wan Chai. You can't deal with both of us. It will ultimately end badly. Make a choice and make it now. Either we have a deal or we don't."

Long is taking a chance, without Montoya he loses his cocaine business. He's betting on his up-and-coming status as the next powerful Dragon Head to have some influence. Benson Yeung is old. His time as leader of the Hong Mian is running out. Without Benson, the leadership goes to his son Henry, and Long doesn't see him as much of a challenge, especially if he's dead.

Alejandro: "If I agree to your ultimatum, Benson Yeung and the lovely Agent Mee Fields will not be happy."

Long: "Don't you worry about Yeung and Fields. Dead people don't squawk."

Sonya Montoya has been sitting listening to the conversation. She's already interrupted once, but she can't sit still for this nonsense. Making a deal with the Wan Chai to go against the Hong Mian is crazy. His plan for supreme triad power is a pipe dream. If a choice had to be made, it made more sense to side with the powerful Hong Mian and their friends in both the British and American governments. Charlie Long was just a mid-level wannabe thug. And besides she didn't like the way he was looking at her, but she resists speaking right out.

She clearly remembers her father smacking her in front of Stone and his friends. She resented the reprimand, not just because it hurt, but because it made her lose face in front of Stone. This time she'd be more discreet. She leans forward and whispers in her father's ear. She tells him Long's plan to kill Benson Yeung and Mee Fields is crazy.

Sonya: *"Papá, no confíes en él. Este plan es locura."* She continues in English, "He underestimates Henry Yeung, and what about Johnny Luck?"

Alejandro looks at his daughter without saying a word. She recognizes the look. She'll be punished later, but at least it won't be in front of Long and his bodyguard.

Alejandro: "You are right my friend, too many cooks in the kitchen spoils the tamales. You get rid of the other cooks and we got a deal."

**Sonya Makes A Move**

# 11
## Sonya Makes A Move

Sonya sits in front of the makeup mirror almost afraid to remove her oversized sunglasses. The beating her father gave her after the meeting with Charlie Long was the worse yet. She removes the glasses. The whole left side of her face is red and swollen; a ring of purple surrounds her left eye; her entire face hurts. No amount of makeup would cover these bruises. Even her lunatic father knew he went too far. He warns her to stay in her room until her face begins to heal.

The temporary confinement has given her time to think. She has had enough; the time has come for her to make a move. Her father made a mistake by letting her run the day-to-day operations. He hasn't been involved in the actual nitty-gritty for quite some time. He spends his days playing the big bad cartel boss, but even then she's at every important meeting, even if she's kept relatively silent. When all is said and done, she is the one that runs things; she is the one the workers' respect. They fear her father, but their loyalty is to her. Despite all his glad-handing, everyone knows Alejandro Montoya is a volatile, violent, son-of-a-bitch.

Sonya has been biding her time for a while. She isn't a child anymore; she's a mature woman that knows how to operate a manufacturing and distribution business, one that specializes in the export of cocaine. She knows all the contacts, and they all know her. The smart ones realize who makes things work. It's Sonya they call if there's a problem, not her father.

Charlie Long's plan to take out the entire leadership of the most powerful triad in North America is bound to end in disaster; and murdering a Section Six Agent is just plain nuts. Even if it was desirable, which it is not, the logistics of doing it are literally impossible. Each target would have to be killed within minutes of one another so that alerts couldn't be sent. Killing Johnny Luck, Benson and Henry Yeung in LA, Stanley Yufu in Toronto, and Mee Fields in London within minutes of one another is a fantasy. This isn't *The God Father*. This is real, deadly real. And what about Mee's estranged husband in LA, The Tailor? The couple may be separated by thousands of miles, but that wouldn't stop the notorious hitman from exacting vengeance… retaliation with extreme prejudice.

Charlie Long's plan is crazy. It would bring down the entire operation. Sonya is not going to let that happen even if it means going against her father. He would have to be retired: retired in a manner in keeping with the changing of the criminal guard. There is no other way. She has suffered her last beating at the hands of her tyrant papa. The King will have to die, long live the Queen, the Queen of Cacaloxuchitl.

Sonya opens her dresser drawer and removes a cell phone kept for just such occasions. She punches in a number. The phone rings several times before a woman answers, "Identify yourself…"

Sonya: "Jesse, we have to talk, it's Sonya. There's trouble coming."

Jesse listens carefully while Sonya fills her in on the meeting between Charlie Long and her father. During the call Johnny Luck and a familiar face enter her office. Jesse's eyes go straight to the other man, they lock eyes like lasers, burning deep and hot. Her free hand instinctively reaches for the ever-present pearl-handled switchblade in her boot. Johnny steps in front of William Stone blocking Jesse's view. He leans over the side of the desk and gently takes the knife out of Jesse's hand. He silently mouths the word, "Behave!" Jesse thanks Sonya for the warning and assures her that when the dust settles, they'll still have a deal, only with Sonya in charge. Jesse hangs up.

Jesse: "FUCK YOU STONE!" Jesse jumps out of her chair practically knocking Johnny into one of the two large framed Botero lithographs hanging on her wall. She grabs Stone by the neck, squeezing hard; then she kisses him even harder. When she's done, she steps back and looks at him with tears in her eyes, "I should cut your fuck'n heart out."

Johnny: "You can do that later, right now we got problems." Jesse tries to compose herself, "I know... Sonya filled me in. When this is over, she's taking control. She'll need our help to take out her old man." Johnny reaches for the phone to call Mo Fields and have him meet them at Benson Yeung's office in The Green Dragon Restaurant.

Stone: "I'm sorry Jesse, I knew it would come to this and... I just wanted to protect you."

Jesse: "I don't need your goddamn protection, I just need you... asshole." The last remark was feeble, almost apologetic. She couldn't stay angry with him, her heart just wasn't in it, but that didn't mean she'd let him off the hook. She'd make him pay: somehow, sometime, but not now; now they had a *Coup d'éte* to put down.

Johnny interrupts, "Okay you two, enough with the lover's quarrel. We have work to do, and Benson expects us in his office in twenty minutes."

Jesse looks at Stone. She squeezes his hand a lot harder than was needed to get the point across. "Later soldier boy... we'll talk later."

**The Lyceum Hit**

# 12
## The Lyceum Hit

The strain of a long distance relationship has taken its toll on the Fields' marriage. With Mo Fields working in Los Angeles and Mee head-quartered in London it was only a matter of time before the marriage fell apart. They still loved each other, but that wasn't enough; not even their daughter Betty could keep their marriage together. A hitman-tailor and a foreign intelligence agent living thousands of miles apart didn't make for a viable relationship. Neverthe-less, Mo would do anything, including risking his life to protect Mee.

One successful assassination is difficult; complet-ing five simultaneously across an ocean and two continents is wishful thinking, but that wasn't going to stop Charlie Long. He's determined to wrestle control away from Benson Yeung no mat-ter what it takes. It's an all-or-nothing gamble, for a man who brags he doesn't gamble. Mee Fields had to go. The triad drug war is about to begin.

Mo Fields goes directly to the airport as soon as the meeting with his Hong Mian superiors is con-cluded. Before he left for the meeting, he threw a suitcase in the trunk of his Lexus. He always kept a bag packed and ready to go on a moments no-tice. No matter what happened at the meeting,

Mo knew he'd be in play; but this was different, this was about Mee.

Henry Young called ahead arranging for one of their London contacts to meet Mo at the airport with a car and a gun as well as any assistance he required. Fields kept trying to get in touch with his wife but she wasn't answering. She was working day and night keeping tabs on a seemingly unemployed post graduate computer-scientist with a lifestyle way beyond his supposed indigent means, a lifestyle that included a drop-dead gorgeous Chinese bombshell that divided her time between the geek's bed and her office at a Chinese News Agency, a well-known front for the Chinese MSS (the Ministry of State Security). Normally this kind of internal surveillance would be a job for the boys in Section Five, but Mee Field's background, heritage, and contacts, plus her fluency in both Mandarin and Cantonese made her the perfect fly-on-the-wall choice.

**11:13 PM BST, London England**
Alfred Hitchcock, the master of movie suspense once remarked, "Drama is life with the dull bits cut out." And so it is that gangsters and spies, like most people, live a very ordinary, mundane existence except for sporadic bouts of violence and intrigue. Heroes and villains eat, sleep, and have sex just like everybody else, and nobody knows that better than a professional killer.

When people get whacked, it happens while they're taking out the garbage, getting a haircut, or enjoying a nice dinner in a neighborhood restaurant. Leave the flashy stuff to the street gangs; those guys always get caught; the real professionals just go about their business identifying routine and striking when it's least expected. And what could be more mundane than going to the theatre where the only people that get killed are the actors. Then again Abraham Lincoln might disagree.

When Fields arrives in London, there's a small middle-aged Chinese woman waiting for him holding a sign with "Moshe Fields" hand-written on it. Mo approaches the woman who grabs his bag and orders him to follow, "Let's go Moshe, we're in a hurry, the theatre gets out in twenty minutes." Mo doesn't bother to correct her, after all, that's what his father called him; he thought Mo was a name for a *shaygetz*.

Mo: "The theatre... why are we going to the theatre?" She doesn't answer.

The little woman practically runs through the terminal toward the parking garage where she's parked a black Jaguar XE. When they get to the car, she opens the boot and throws Mo's bag in. She retrieves a brown paper bag and slams it into Mo's chest, "Let's go Moshe, we got to get to the Lyceum before it let's out. They get in the car with the woman driving. She tear-asses out of the parking level paying no attention to one-way signs or directions, when she gets to the parking attendant's booth she slams on the brakes coming to an abrupt halt only inches from the barrier. She flashes some kind of badge and the attendant immediately opens the gate. She hits the gas pedal and quickly shifts through the gears until she's traveling well beyond the speed limit. Mo looks in the bag, He removes the chamois wrapped Glock 17 and the separate suppressor. He sticks the Glock in a specially re-enforced inner pocket on the inside of his suit jacket, being a tailor has its advantages. He sticks the suppressor in his outside jacket pocket.

Cookie: "You can call me Cookie. Your ex-wife is tailing some Cambridge computer geek working for Chinese intelligence. The hacker is making contact with his handler at the theatre. When the performance is over, they'll be the usual crowd milling about in front of the theatre. That's when I figure Long plans to take her out. They'll make it fast and loud and try to get away in the confusion. I've got two men watching the entrance and one inside the lobby. The problem is we don't know the shooter. He… or she could be anyone."

The trip from Heathrow Airport to the Lyceum normally takes twenty-seven minutes; they make it in less than twenty despite the heavy London traffic. The Lyceum wraps around the corner of Wellington and Exeter. Cookie brings the Jag to a screeching halt beside the theatre on the Exeter side. People are just beginning to exit. In a few minutes it will be total bedlam. Cookie uses the phone in the car to try to get in touch with her people. There's no answer. Mo spots two drunks asleep in an alcove ten feet from where they're parked. Mo points, "Is that them?"

Cookie: "Shit!" She jumps out of the car almost getting hit by a passing cab. She races to the alcove with Mo Fields right behind her. She squats down beside one of the men and removes the Kangol cap covering his head revealing a small caliber hole right above the ear. She looks up at Mo.

Mo: "This one's dead too."

Cookie: "Let's find these fuckers."

Mo and Cookie enter the theatre. Cookie looks around but can't find her other colleague in the confusion. Mo scans the lobby but can't find Mee.

Mee has hung back in her seat as the theatre empties except for a few people waiting for the rush to subside. Her targets are sitting about ten rows in front of her and off to the right. Mee sees the computer boffin and the pretty Chinese agent get up and head for the side exit that leads to the sidewalk on Exeter. She gets up to follow. A young usher approaches Mee as she reaches the exit just after the door closes behind the hacker and his handler.

Usher: "Let me get the door for you." The usher steps in front of Mee grabbing the door handle with one hand as he reaches into his usher's uniform jacket with the other removing a Sig-Sauer Semi-Automatic. He opens the door for Mee. As she steps on to the sidewalk, he puts two slugs in the back of her head, the door closes behind her as she tumbles to the ground dead.

**Yufu Must Die**

# 13
## Yufu Must Die

**6:30 EST, Toronto, Ontario**

For Charlie Long's plan to work the entire leadership of the Hong Mian must be eliminated, and that includes Stanley Yufu, the head of Canadian operations. The Chinese Jack Palance look-alike works out of several offices depending on what particular operation needs his personal attention.

Yufu and his newly appointed second-in-command, Kenny Kang, handle the distribution and export of ecstasy, run two Southern Ontario racetracks, and handle Toronto's most extensive loan shark and gambling operation. In short, next to Benson Yeung, his son Henry, and Johnny Luck, Stanley Yufu is the most powerful Hong Mian leader in North America. If the other three were eliminated, Yufu would be in line to succeed as Dragon Head.

Yufu divides his time between the Woodbridge racetrack on the outskirts of Toronto and the Crystal Beach track located next to Fort Erie. It's Thursday and Yufu is in Crystal Beach checking on the horses being readied to mule this week's batch of 'Happy Pills' to the triad's Italian partners, the Fungo Family. While Jesse was running the Crystal Beach operation she came up with the ingenious plan of using broodmares to smuggle the drugs.

Broodmares often undergo a surgical procedure called the Caslick, named after the veterinarian that came up with the procedure designed to protect broodmares from infection. It involves surgically closing the upper part of the vulva. Jesse came up with the idea of loading the drugs into the animal's uterus before it's sewn closed. Once loaded, the horses are sold and transported to friendly horse farms located throughout the US in strategically located areas. The drugs are then removed and distributed.

After checking on the horses, Yufu is scheduled to have lunch with Nicky Fungo, at their newest local money-laundering asset, Fang and Feinstein's Fine Food: a combination Jewish deli and Chinese food mash-up that is sure to alienate any politically correct purist worried about cultural appropriation. It seems war has broken out between the two nominal owners Billy Fang and Levi Feinstein. It seems their dispute revolves around the naming of the customer-favorite meat-filled dumplings. Should they be listed on the Chinese side of the menu as wontons, or on the deli side of the menu as kreplach.  The fact that Stanley Yufu ran a large criminal operation involved in all kinds of nefarious enterprises didn't insulate him from the mundane management problems resulting from employing human beings.

Yufu, Kang, and Nicky Fungo enter the packed restaurant and are greeted by a barrage of scatological Chinese and equally profane Yiddish coming from the kitchen. Half the diners pay no attention to the tumult coming from the kitchen while the other half find the cultural war of insults amusing; an entertaining extra, added to the lunchtime experience. Yufu suggests Kang and Fungo take their seats while he attempts to quell the epicurean revolution, but the two gangsters want to see what all the fuss is about. They follow their host through the swinging doors that lead to the heart of the menu naming kerfuffle. All the cooks are busy preparing meals while Fang and Feinstein verbally duke it out in the middle of the kitchen.

Yufu: "What the hell is going on here?"

Fang points a finger into Feinstein's face, "*Tā shìgè báichī, tāmen shì bèndàn!*"

Yufu: "English... Fang... speak English, he doesn't know what the hell you're saying."

Fang: "He's an idiot, they're wontons, not kreplach."

Feinstein: "*Momzer*... Get your finger out of my face. *Gey strashe di gens!*"

In the corner, one of the dishwashers continually washes the same twelve-inch meat cleaver seemingly distracted from his duties by the argument and the arrival of Yufu and the two other big shots.

Fungo: "Is that what this argument is about… kreplach or wantons? Don't you two dummies know they're ravioli?"

Fang and Feinstein both stop, turn, and simultaneously speak, "Who the fuck are you?"

Fungo: "I should have brought my piece, that would shut you two numbskulls up."

Kang chimes in: "I did." He reaches into his suit jacket and removes a Smith and Wesson semi automatic. Everyone in the kitchen stops what they're doing and looks at Kang with his gun raised above his shoulder. There's a split second of silence that's broken by the dishwasher screaming some unintelligible gibberish as he charges towards Stanley Yufu waving the cleaver wildly in the air. Kang lowers his piece and shoots, putting a bullet in the center of the dishwasher's forehead. He takes one more step towards Yufu and falls face first on the tile floor.

Feinsten looks down at the dead body of Charlie Long's dishwasher assassin: "… *Lign in dred un bakn beygl!*"

Fang looks at Yufu: "What are we supposed to do with him?" Before Yufu can answer Fungo breaks the silence: "You can always chop him up in little pieces and stuff him in the fucking wanton-kreplach. Just don't call them ravioli."

**And The Hits Keep Coming**

# 14
## And The Hits Keep Coming

There are different kinds of hits: murders that make a statement, splashy, extravagant performances that send a message: the St. Valentine's Day Massacre being one of the most infamous and perhaps messiest. And then there are the more subtle takeouts, murders that quietly and hopefully without notice eliminate an obstacle that stands in the way of progress: take, for instance, the slow moving murder of Georgi Ivanov Markov, a Bulgarian dissident jabbed in the leg by an umbrella wielded by a Bulgarian secret agent that used the brolly to deliver a deadly injection of ricin. Commit the right kind of murder, right being a rather elusive concept in this context, and you just might get away with it. Screw-up and you may find yourself divided into manageable chunks stuffed into green garbage bags along with some heavy ballast to avoid unexpectedly popping up along the LA waterfront.

**3:30 PST, Los Angeles, California**
Benson Yeung, his eldest son Henry, Zack Wei, and Genghis Lee are enjoying a late dim sum lunch in the Green Dragon Restaurant. Once a month Wei and Lee report on the month's results, and if there are any issues with the authorities or the rival Wan Chai. Despite being central to the whole operation, Stone is not at the meeting. He maintains the persona of a wealthy absentee owner more interested in his South Amer-

ican art gallery hobby than in his majority position in the Murphy Peanut Butter Company. His money laundering manipulations can be handled from anywhere in the world as long as he has access to a computer and an Internet connection. The dirty business of drug trafficking is left to the experts; his specialty is moving money in an international high-stakes game of Three-card Monte. Stone's only regular operational contact is with Zack Wei who runs the Murphy operation, thereby eliminating any needless Hong Mian communication. But Stone had no choice but to tell Johnny Luck about Charlie Long's surprise visit to the *La Galeria de Rosa,* confirming Sonya Montoya's warning about the Wan Chai plot. With his Hong Mian obligation done, his priority is reconnecting with Jesse.

While Wei, Lee, and the Bensons enjoy lunch, Jesse, Stone and Luck gather around the back-stretch barn of Devil Beast, the horse Jesse purchased in a claiming race a year earlier when she and Stone where in Argentina. Devil Beast is what some would call crowbait, in other words, it's not a very good-looking horse. There is still tension between Jesse and Stone but the relationship is quickly returning to their comfortable pattern of friendly ribbing.

Stone looks at Devil Beast and then at Jesse: "I thought you ripped-off Juan Pedro not the other way around. That's *un caballo feo*!"

Jesse: "You forget I speak a little Spanish too, so fuck you. This horse can run. Besides the great unwashed take one look at him and think he's a loser, even if the Racing Form says otherwise." Her hand finds Stone's. She gently squeezes easing the bite of her tone.

A Mexican hot walker comes out of the stall next to Devil Beasts'. He looks at Johnny Luck and in a heavy Spanish accent asks, "*¿Eres Johnny Suerte?*"

Johnny turns and looks at the guy, "Yeah, I'm Mister Luck, how can I help you?"

Mexican: "I got a message for you from Mr. Montoya and *Señor Largo*…" At first it doesn't register on Luck that he's talking about Montoya and Charlie Long. Why would Montoya send him a message delivered by some unknown stable hand? All communication from Montoya went through Wei or Genghis Lee. And who the hell is *Largo*?

Luck: "So what's the message?" The Mexican moves his hand to the small of his back, but he hesitates just for a second, long enough for Jesse to reach down into her boot for her pearl handled switchblade. As the Mexican brings the Hi-Point C9 semi-automatic around, Jesse straightens up, and in one violent underhanded motion flicks her pearl handled blade in the direction of the Mexican, catching him on the side of the neck close enough to the carotid artery to do maximum damage.

The Mexican falls to his knees grasping his neck with one hand while still holding the gun with his other. Blood erupts from his neck in long dark red streams.

Johnny walks up to the dying Mexican, "Montoya and Charlie Long sent you?" The Mexican tries to raise the gun towards Luck as he continues in a feeble attempt to stem the flow of blood with his other hand. Luck gently takes the gun out of the Mexican's hand, places it close to his forehead and fires.

He turns to Jesse: "Clean this up for me, and send what's left to the pig farm."

Back in front of the Green Dragon six shiny green Kawasaki ZZR1400 motorcycles roar up to the front of the restaurant. Inside, the Bensons, Wei, and Genghis Lee are finishing lunch. The restaurant is busy with the clatter of dishes and chatter of patrons making it unlikely that anyone notices the six heavily armed, green-clad gang members that burst through the front doors.

Their green leather jackets each feature a yellow lightning bolt on the back. All six intruders are carrying automatic machine pistols and wearing black stocking masks. They push their way past the attractive hostess knocking her to the floor, tearing her tight silk cheongsam.

Shots are fired into the ceiling scaring the civilians causing a stampede for the front door. The invading thugs spot the Bensons, Wei, and Lee. Henry tries to cover his father while pushing the elderly Dragon Head towards the kitchen. Henry takes a bullet in the leg just as he pushes his father through the swinging kitchen doors. They both go down in a heap on the floor.

Wei and Lee push over the table for cover; they draw their weapons and return fire. Several cooks come charging out of the kitchen all firing automatic weapons. When the dust settles Zack Wei and Genghis Lee both sustain non-life-threatening wounds. Two of the cooks are also shot, but the invaders are all killed. Wei takes a bullet in the arm, and Lee is nicked by a slug to his thigh.

Wei and Lee approach the bodies on the floor and remove their stocking masks one at a time. Wei looks at Lee, "Who the fuck are these clowns?" Lee looks, "They're Wan Chai soldiers, members of the *Jiangshi* Motorcycle Gang." The lightning bolt is their signature.

The war for control of the Montoya Special Brand Chili has begun.

**The Revenge Summit**

## 15
## The Revenge Summit

The Green Dragon is out of commission. The restaurant will have to be completely renovated but not until the authorities have finished investigating it as a crime scene. The place is crawling with local police and the FBI, each bickering over jurisdiction, collecting evidence, and trolling for intelligence on the Hong Mian.

None of the survivors say a word; they deny knowing who the shooters were and why they attacked. Revenge would be meted out privately and without concern for the authorities. Since the Green Dragon was off limits, everyone met in Johnny Luck's office at the Hancock complex in the Shanghai Player's Club. Benson and Henry Yeung led the meeting attended by Luck, Jesse, Stone, Wei, Lee and Mo Fields.

As they are about to begin Mo Fields stands and speaks: "I'll do whatever needs to be done, but Charlie Long is mine. It's not just business, it's personal." Everyone turns to Benson Yeung to hear the Dragon Head's reaction.

You don't make demands on the boss, but Benson nods his head. "Mo my friend, you've been a loyal soldier for years and you deserve your pound of flesh. The murder of your lovely wife was totally out of line and must be avenged, and you'll have your chance, but we need a plan."

Stone speaks: "Long's got this setup at the Happy Hills Racetrack. He's had his men install some kind of contraption under the starting gate that fires tranquilizer darts from a remote location, maybe from the stands or even somewhere in the track office. He can fix any race, guaranteeing a winner any time he wants. If we have one of our people accidentally discover the device and inform our contacts in the local police department that would be enough for them to make an arrest."

Luck: "How does that help? He'll be behind bars and unreachable. Besides, he has friends in the department too, and dozens of lawyers. He'll be out in forty-eight hours, guaranteed."

Fields: "Don't worry about that, you just get me in and out, and I'll do the rest."

Stone: "Maybe the Wan Chai can survive a race track scandal, but if Mo pops him in prison, it will create a real shit-storm. The authorities will have no choice but to investigate, but if we smuggle Mo in and out of the country, no one will ever know he was there. The government will assume his own people popped him to shut him up. They'll have no choice but to come down on the entire Wan Chai operation. With Long gone and his organization in disarray, we kill two birds with one Mo Field's stone."

Benson: "Agreed." He turns to his son, "Henry, contact our friends in the HKPF and make the arrangement for Mo."

Jesse: "What about Montoya? We promised Sonya we'd help her eliminate her father."

Luck: "The trick is to get someone he doesn't know close enough to do the job. He knows everybody here so none of us would get close enough."

Jesse: "He doesn't know me. The only one I've had contact with is Sonya. He doesn't do business with women, he barely tolerates his own daughter, but without her he'd be lost."

Stone: "I don't like it, find someone else."

Benson: "No, she's right. It's a good idea. Didn't Sonya go to school at UCLA?"

Henry: "Yes, I think she did, but I can check to make sure."

Jesse: "Perfect, I'm just an old school girlfriend coming for a visit. From what Sonya tells me, the old man likes them young and blonde. It doesn't sound like getting up close and personal will be a problem."

Stone: "Now wait just a minute…"

Luck: "He's right. We're putting Jesse in a tight spot. That's not her job."

Benson: "Her job, like everyone else in this room is to do what I tell them. It's decided. Jesse, make the arrangement with Sonya." Stone tries to object again but Benson just raises his hand. "I understand everyone's concern, but Jesse is a big girl, and she knows how to handle herself."

Henry: "Maybe Stone could show up at the same time to discuss what to do about the Long mess. That way she'd have some back-up other than Sonya's people."

Benson thinks for a moment. "Agreed, Stone can go as backup on the pretext of discussing Long's failed Coup."

Lee: "What about the *Jiangshi* bastards? They need to be taught a lesson. Anybody got any ideas?"

Jesse: "Why don't you Sokolov them, like the Israelis did to Giacometti? Wait till it's dark and have your boys drop a few drones loaded with C4 on the roof."

Benson: "I'll leave that business to Genghis. I assume the Lion Dogs can handle it?"

Genghis nods, "Absolutely! We'll send those *Húndàn* a message they won't forget."

**King Kong vs. Genghis The Khan Lee**

# 16
## King Kong vs. Genghis The Khan Lee

The *Jiangshi* Motorcycle Club gets its name from the ancient Chinese legend of reanimated dead bodies known as the *Jiangshi*. The name is meant to symbolize the idea that no enemy can kill a club member as he is already dead. It's a ridiculous but powerful metaphysical mental gymnastic that convinces club members they are impervious to rival attacks.

Their green leather jackets feature a yellow lightning bolt as its signature logo. According to legend, a *Jiangshi* is created when a corpse is struck by lightning or when a pregnant cat leaps over its coffin. The choice of a lightning bolt seemed more dramatic than a pregnant cat.

Their clubhouse is the re-purposed bankrupt Black Tiger Chinese Restaurant. The green and yellow pagoda style roof matches the green-painted stucco façade with a giant yellow lightning bolt slashing across the front entrance as if bisecting the carved ornate wooden doors.

The place did not give off a welcoming appearance. It generally had a minimum of a dozen green Kawasaki low-rider motorcycles parked out front along with a group of large tattooed Chinese men that you would not want to meet at night in a dark alley.

The leader of the *Jiangshi* is a fifty-year-old giant that goes by the name of Tommy Kong, and of course his colleagues called him King. A shaved head the size of one of those award-winning pumpkins tops Tommy's six-foot-seven, three hundred pound frame. His face features the largest, thickest, and bushiest white Fu Manchu mustache you'll ever see. All in all, Tommy King Kong is one scary looking motherfucker.

It's a normal weekday afternoon in the City of Angels, a town known as much for self-help charlatans, quinoa salads, and silicone boobs, as it is for sunshine, movie stars, and earthquakes that might make Arizona a coastal state. People are shopping, dining on outdoor patios, and having drinks while plotting their next big career move, illicit affair, or in the case of Genghis Lee, revenge.

An LAPD police cruiser pulls up in front of the *Jiangshi* clubhouse. A half a dozen club members mill about outside the heavily carved doors, guarding the entrance, while keeping an eye on their signature low-riders. They laugh and poke one another in the arm as they see the cops stop only inches from scraping the paint on Tommy Kong's cherished possession. The driver gets out of the cop car banging the door into Tommy's bike. The gang members begin to close in on the cop but a second more senior Police Sergeant gets out of the passenger seat, "Back the fuck off!" The gang members do as they're told.

The driver opens the back door of the cruiser and Genghis Lee, dressed in a Mo Fields tropical wool special steps out, leaving behind a black leather attaché case. The senior cop and Lee walk past the *Jiangshi* soldiers and enter the building. The place is filled with tables and a long fancy bar just like it was when it functioned as a public restaurant. Now it only serves *Jiangshi* and friends. Several senior club members occupy the bar.

Sitting in a booth in the back of the restaurant is Tommy Kong and two of his lieutenants. The cop and Lee walk directly to Kong's table while the rest of the room eyeballs the intruders. The cop looks at one of the gang members seated at a table next to the booth, "Get the fuck off the chair!" The club member looks at Kong who nods. He gets up and leaves but not before spewing a few colorful verbal retorts. The cop places the chair in front of the table opposite Tommy Kong. Genghis sits down.

Kong: "How's the hip?"

Lee: "Hurts like a bitch."

Kong: "Could've been a lot worse."

Lee: "Yeah, I could've ended up like your guys. I guess that lightning bolt *shtick* doesn't work indoors."

Kong looks at the cop standing arms cross behind Lee. He shrugs. "I see you brought one of your pet pigs." The cop responds with a smirk.

Lee: "You see Tommy, that's what makes us different. We've adapted to a new order. We have friends… We've matured, grown out of our street gang mentality, we're businessmen, whereas you're still… a punk."

Kong: "Yeah, I get it. You've become a pussy in an expensive suit. So what are you doing here? You wouldn't have brought Sergeant Oink if you meant business. You waving the white flag?"

Lee: "Charlie Long and the Wan Chai are finished. They overstepped their bounds, but you and your men have a way out. Join us and you'll be protected. You'll make more money without the concern of retaliation. One-time offer my friend. Take it or leave it."

Kong: "I'll discuss it with the boys and get back to you in twenty-four hours."

Genghis gets up, "It's a good deal Tommy. Be smart. Charlie Long's a cooked goose."

Kong laughs, "I think you mean a dead duck."

Lee: "What I mean is, he's fucked!"

Lee and the cop leave the clubhouse. The *Jiangshi* thugs are still outside staring-down the police-driver. Genghis gets into the back of the cruiser and the Sergeant gets into the front passenger seat. The driver opens the driver-side door abruptly smashing it into Tommy Kong's motor-cycle, knocking it over with a large dent and scrape on the fuel tank. The thugs start yelling obscenities as the cop car drives off.

The cop travels about twenty yards down the street when Genghis removes his cell phone from the breast pocket of his suit. He dials a number and enters a code. Fifteen seconds later as the cop car turns the corner there's a series of huge explosions. The Police Sergeant turns to look at Genghis, "I thought you were going to give him twenty-four hours."

Lee: "Fuck'em! He shot me and tried to kill the old man. He got what he deserved."

Sergeant: "This isn't what was agreed."

Lee picks up the attaché case he left sitting on the back seat of the cruiser. He hands it to the cop. "It is now."

The cop opens the attaché case that is filled with neat stacks of hundred-dollar bills. He closes the brief case. "The guy was an asshole, anyway."

**Dead Men Don't Die**

## 17
## Dead Men Don't Die

The *LA News Reporter's* headline screams out in large black type:

**"Chinatown Gas Explosion Kills,
The Body Count Yet To Be Determined"**

The article goes on to describe how the bankrupt Black Tiger Restaurant was being used by the *Jiangshi* Motorcycle Club for various nefarious purposes. The authorities insist on blaming the disaster on a poorly maintained furnace, but nobody really believes it. There's a not very subtle implication that the explosion was more likely the beginning of a Chinatown gang war.

Fire Marshal Wilson MacAvoy and his hand-picked crew, fresh from depositing large sums of money in their safety deposit boxes, arrive on the scene almost immediately after the explosion. They cordon off Broadway from Bernard Street to College Street, even limiting access to the police and other officials on the pretext that the area is still potentially dangerous. No one was allowed near the Black Tiger to recover the bodies until the inspector's crew had collected and destroyed whatever drone evidence survived the blasts.

One of the firemen approaches his boss after several hours of late night rummaging through what was left of the restaurant.

Fireman: "I heard some moaning coming from the bathroom. I think there's a survivor."

Fire Marshal: "Shit… you just can't kill these fuckers."

Fireman: "What should we do?"

Fire Marshal: "You think you got everything that we need to collect."

Fireman: "I think so, but shit, in this mess, it's hard to tell. What do you want to do about the moaner?"

Fire Marshal: "Can we get to him?" The fireman nods. "Okay… Show me." The two men pick their way through the wreckage making their way to the bathrooms in the rear of the building. At one point a beam comes down just missing the Fire Marshal. The two men stop, hold their breath, and carefully move toward the back. There's debris blocking the entrance to the bathroom door. It's too heavy and too dangerous for the two men to move it. There's a hole in the bottom of the door under the rubble with just enough room for someone to get their head in.

Fireman: "You want me to take a look?"

Fire Marshal: "Just be careful. You get killed and this whole shit-storm will come apart."

The fireman has to remove his helmet in order to fit under the caved-in ceiling parts. The Fire Marshal shakes his head in anticipation of the danger. The fire fighter gets down on his hands and knees and wedges himself under the debris where the hole in the door is located. The moans from the bathroom become louder. As the fireman works his way into the cramped opening, he nudges a fallen ceiling beam with his shoulder; the beam shifts causing more drywall and roof tiles to come down; both men freeze. The fireman continues carefully moving towards the opening; he looks through the hole in the door.

Fireman: "Fuck…" It's almost a whisper. There's a man sitting on the toilet with his pants around his legs. Blood drips down his huge bald head from where the ceiling tiles decided to break their fall. The red ooze seeps across his massive forehead over his bruised cheeks and into his bushy white moustache, turning it a dark dirty red.

Fire Marshal: "Who is it?"

Fireman: "Tommy Kong"

Fire Marshal: "God damn it. I told you: you can't kill these bastards." The Fire Marshal takes a few steps away from the door and retrieves his cell phone from his jacket pocket. He dials a number.

A voice answers on the other end. It's the Police Sergeant that accompanied Genghis Lee to the *Jiangshi* clubhouse.

Fire Marshal: "The fucker is still alive."

At about the same time, three Wan Chai soldiers arrive in Palermo, Argentina. When asked at immigration what the purpose was of their visit, they say they're there to visit an art gallery that specializes in selling Botero lithographs.

**Playing The Odds**

# 18
## Playing The Odds

Cookie sits in an oversized silk and linen upholstered chair that dwarfs her petite black clad body. Her arms rest on the shiny black wooden frame made from one of those exotic South American endangered species. Her silk pajama-style pantsuit cut in the traditional Chinese fashion with the high-neck collar jacket makes her look like a rich matron more interested in the Peninsula's famous afternoon tea service than in deadly revenge. Cookie looks out the expanse of double-glazed glass into the harbour. She watches as one of the ferries crosses from Hong Kong to Kowloon where The Peninsula Hotel calls home.

Although the suite seems to be an oasis of peace, tranquility, and wealth, it is, in fact, abuzz with activity. At each end of what was once a long dining room table, are two young men surrounded by four computer monitors. On either side of the table, are two attractive women each with laptops and printers. Fingers dance across the keyboards in a never-ending rhythmic search for information. The digital dance is periodically punctuated by curt Chinese declarations delivered without emotion, but with an obvious sense of urgency. When a printer spews forth its magic, one of the women delivers it to one of the two Australian men sitting across from Cookie.

Cookie is still upset about her failure to stop the Wan Chai from killing Mee Fields. Cookie was Mee's mentor and friend. She wanted revenge for Mee's death almost as much as Mo. Her demand for retribution created such a stink in Section Six that she was suspended with pay for a month. The pompous bastards that hide in the panelled thirty-sixth floor offices said it was for her own good; time to cool off and get her head straight; but her head was straight. It was so fucking straight she knew exactly what she had to do, whether those pinched-lipped, public school cowards liked it or not.

Sure there was a week indulging in too much cheesecake and gin, but then the call came from Johnny Luck. She could've kissed him if he wasn't thousands of miles away. Fuck the Section Six sycophants; she'd do this off the books.

There's a call from the front desk. Carson Mimes has arrived, and he is on his way up to the suite. A few minutes later there's a knock on the door. One of the young women jumps from her station and briskly walks to the door, opens it, wheels around, and returns to her duties.

Mo Fields walks in. He takes a seat beside Cookie in a matching chair. The Australians across from Cookie barely notice. They return to their laptops and enter the results after consulting each new printout delivered by their associates.

Cookie's hand reaches over and touches Mo's: "How have you been?"

Mo: "Getting by. This operation may help."

Cookie nods in agreement. "What's your handle this time?"

Mo: "Carson Mimes… a bit pretentious if you ask me, but that's what they gave me. So what's the play?"

Cookie: "These two computer cowboys are the Duffy brothers: Darcy and Derek." Neither brother looks up. "Don't ask me which one is which. I just call them Doofus and Dipshit." She looks up at the brothers. "Hay Doofus and Dipshit; it's time to stop fucking around and get to work."

Darcy: "What do you think…"

Derek: "…we're doing."

Cookie looks at Mo. "Cute. The two nerds actually finish each other's sentences." Darcy and Derek go back to work.

Mo: "So what's the deal?"

Cookie: "Our friends in the HKPF weren't too eager to lose those Charlie Long care packages at the end of each month, but it seems your boss promised to replace their losses plus a bonus:

kind of an American style repeal-and-replace thing. That seemed to change their minds, but they still insisted we provide some evidence of hanky-panky. The cops just can't show up at Happy Hills with shovels and start digging up the track. They need an excuse. That's what these two clowns are trying to find. They're computer-assisted horse bettors."

Mo: "That's a thing?"

Cookie: "Goddamn right it's a thing. This room generates close to a million dollars a week in profits. They analyze every horse that runs at Happy Hills, twelve hundred horses. They know every fucking thing about these horses, and not just the stuff in the racing forms. If a horse takes a loose dump, they know it. Then they filter all the data through some top-secret algorithm and come up with a number; they're looking for 'positive expectations'.

Say for example their data tells them a horse running at 10-1 has a .1 probability of winning. You multiply the 10 times the .1 and come up with 1-1, an even-money bet, but if that same horse is running at 15-1 the positive expectation becomes 1.5-1 or a fifty percent better bet.

What our boys are doing is analyzing all the races this year to see if they can find a pattern where horses with high odds and low probability had significant shifts in odds in the final hours before a race, and ended up winning.

Some long shot starts off at 50-1 but drops to 45-1 just before race time; that means somebody dumped a lot of money on a loser, but it wins. Nobody thinks twice about it, it happens, but if the boys can find a consistent pattern over time, that's evidence. I hand that sucker over to the HKPF and *voila* they got their excuse. They nose around and what do you think they find, a buried dart delivery system under the starting gate."

One of the women jumps up from her computer and races across the room handing each brother a sheet of paper. The brothers look at the papers and enter a bunch of numbers in their laptops. The woman stands over them waiting. Her colleagues have all stopped working and are watching. The two brothers both stop and stare at their screens. They turn to each other, smile, and awkwardly high-five. They turn back to look at Cookie and Mo.

Darcy: "BINGO Motherfucker!"

Derek: "We got him!"

The printers on the dining room table start to spit out paper. The other young woman carefully puts all the sheets of paper in order and walks them over to the brothers' desk.

Darcy points to Cookie: "Be my..."

Derek: "...guest"

Cookie: "You two clowns should take this act on the road." The young assistant hands Cookie the stack of papers. She looks at the papers and then up at the brothers. "What am I looking at?"

Darcy: "Each line represents a race that your target fixed. You have the day, the race, the odds, and the payout, along with the negative expectation number and the final precipitous and unnoticed drop in odds. It seems that one race per day was fixed, usually the last race. The chances of all these horses winning are literally impossible according to every mathematical model we ran. Sure it can happen a few times every meet but not every race day. It just can't happen. You give that to the cops and your boy is toast."

That night the HKPF Gambling Unit raids the Happy Hills Racetrack and digs up the dirt under the starting gate. Low and behold they find Charlie Long's tranquilizer delivery system. Two hours later, the same squad raids The Laughing Monkey, arresting Charlie Long. He's placed in isolation for his own protection.

**The Cervantes Connection**

**19**
**The Cervantes Connection**

Margarita Cervantes stands on a small stool hanging the last of a series of large pen and colored ink portraits by a local Soho street-artist. The bell on the door signals someone has entered. Margarita turns to look. Trouble has arrived again. Three husky men in ill-fitting suits stand admiring the view of Margarita balancing her lithe young body on the small footstool.

Margarita steps down, taking in the details of each man like William taught her. Two of the men are young with stubble and stupid haircuts. That rules out the possibility of them being *policias*. The other guy is older, at least forty. He is slightly better dressed with moderately improved grooming. Whoever they are, they're not William's friends; and they're not Chinese so they're not the guys that showed up at the gallery threatening William to keep out of whatever they were planning. Whoever they are, they mean business.

The older man speaks in English with a heavy rural Mexican accent. "You're going to have to come with us."

Margarita: "I don't think so."

The two younger creeps just ogle Margarita with silly smirks on their faces. They casually unbutton their ill-fitting suit jackets revealing the automatic weapons dangling from their leather shoulder holsters.

Margarita: "I'll have to call my mother so she can come and look after the gallery."

Older Mexican: "Just lock it up, we're in a hurry."

Margarita: "That's not too bright is it? My parents will worry. Maybe they'll call la *policia*."

Older Mexican: "Not if they're *muerto*, they can't. Your choice: lock it up, or I send my associates across the street to deal with Mama and Papa."

Margarita: "The keys are in the office desk, Can I get them?"

Older Mexican: "Make it fast."

Margarita turns and goes into the back office. She opens William's desk drawer and reaches in for the keys to the front door. She hesitates. Beside the keys is a Glock 30S Compact 45. She looks at the framed photo of Jesse on William's desk. She's in her full riding gear on Medicine Hat, her big Derby win. Perhaps this is Margarita's chance to prove she's every bit the woman Jesse is. She looks through the doorway into the gallery. The two younger men are looking at the artwork while the older guy just stands and waits.

Older Mexican: "*Hazlo rapido!*"

Margarita picks up the keys in her left hand and casually retrieves the Glock with her right. She moves from behind the desk and into the office doorway. William taught her to shoot, but this is different, these are real people, thugs for sure, but still, they're people, not paper targets. She tentatively steps onto the gallery floor and stops. The keys dangle from her left hand while the Glock is hidden behind her back in her right.

Older Mexican: "So, what the hell are you waiting for?"

Margarita brings her right hand around from behind her back as her finger squeezes the trigger; the first slug hits the floor in front of the older Mexican; the second goes into the ceiling caused by the gun's recoil. She gets off one more shot before the older Mexican wrestles her to the ground. He hits her hard across the face knocking her unconscious. He stands up over Margarita's prone body cursing in Spanish under his breath. One of his associates stands with his gun drawn, legs apart, crouched low like something he saw in a Jason Stratham movie. The other thug lies flat on his back in the middle of the gallery floor, blood oozes from his chest. The third shot did its work even though she was aiming at the older Mexican.

That evening when Margarita doesn't come home for dinner, her mother and father go to find out what's keeping her. The gallery is locked. Juan Pedro uses a spare set of keys to enter. He tells his wife to wait outside. She refuses, following him in. When they enter, Juan Pedro turns on the lights. There's a large dark red stain in the middle of the floor.

Maria: "*Madre de Dios! Ellos la mataron.*" She starts to cry.

Juan Pedro: "We don't know it's her blood. Calm down for Christ's sake!"

He sees that the blood trail leads to Stone's office. He follows it. The office is dark. He turns on the light while standing in the doorway. One of the younger Mexicans is propped up in William's chair. His tight-fitting white shirt has been stained dark red from the blood that escaped from the hole in his chest. Maria peeks over her husband's shoulder into the room.

Maria: "*Gracias a Dios.* We should call the police."

Juan Pedro: "Don't be stupid. This *cabron* is fish bait. I'll call William, you clean up that mess on the gallery floor." Juan Pedro reaches for the phone beside the empty picture frame that used to hold a picture of Jesse.

Long's Gone?

## 20
## Long's Gone?

Mo Fields, in the guise of Carson Mimes, Criminal Lawyer, is led down a steep metal stairway into the basement of the local Wan Chai district jail. You wouldn't think a high profile prisoner like Charlie Long would be kept in a place normally reserved for Saturday night drunks and local street brawlers. Fields is more than a bit surprised the OCTB (Organized Crime and Triad Bureau) didn't take control of the situation but instead left it up to the local cops who stashed Long in what amounted to a drunk tank; perhaps that was the plan all along, making it easier for Mo to get in and out without scrutiny from the real professionals in a building with elaborate security.

The basement jail houses two tightly packed rows of cells. The place is old, dank, and smells of Chinese food and urine. The concrete cement walls are painted bilious bile yellow and the almost solid metal doors are an equally unappetizing pea green. Each metal door has a narrow row of bars across the top and bottom so inmates can breathe in the stale humid air and rats can freely roam around looking for snacks.

The name tag on the Police Constable accompanying Mo is Jian Lam, a young man that looks barely old enough to drive let alone carry a gun. His mother must be proud when he leaves the house wearing his crisp light blue short-sleeve shirt and official police uniform hat. When this day is done, Mama may not be so proud, but at least she'll have a substantial increase in her bank balance.

Lam points Mo to Long's cell.  Mo positions himself directly across from the green metal door marked Number 9. He undoes his jacket and reaches behind his back to retrieve the Glock Cookie provided before he entered the building. Lam reaches into his pocket and hands Mo a silencer. Mo screws the suppressor onto the end of the Glock.

The plan is simple. Lam will open the door; Mo will step forward; confirm it's Charlie Long in the cell; then he'll put two slugs in Long's chest and one more between his eyes. The young cop will lock the cell and escort Mo out of the building. How the kid is supposed to wriggle out of the sticky situation is not Mo's concern. Kill Long and get the fuck out. Clean. Simple. And final.

Mo points to the door. Lam sticks the key in the lock and turns. He grabs the metal handle and opens the door as he steps back out of the way. Mo raises the Glock about chest high and steps forward as the sole inmate gets up from a filthy metal cot. Mo looks...

Mo: "Who the fuck are you?" It's not Charlie Long.

The inmate starts babbling something in Chinese as he drops to his knees, assumedly praying or begging for his life.

Mo looks at Lam. "He says he's Charlie Long."

Mo: "That's not Charlie Long, where the hell is Charlie Long?" Mo is calm but angry; the kid is scared he might pay for the fuckup with his own hat trick of slugs. He looks down at the clipboard he's been carrying and runs his finger down the page. "It says here, Cell Number 9, Charlie Long."

Mo: "You assholes got the wrong Charlie Long. Charlie-fucking-Long, Dragon Head of the Wan Chai, and owner of The Laughing-fucking-Monkey. He's the most prominent triad boss on the island. How do you fuck that up?" The kid is scared. He can't even speak.

Mo turns to the kid: "Switch clothes with this loser."

Lam: "I beg your pardon?"

Mo: "Take off your fucking clothes before I put a bullet in both of you idiots."

Lam and the inmate switch clothes. Mo orders Lam into the cell.

Mo: "Anybody asks, Long overpowered you, knocked you unconscious, and escaped. Got it?" The kid nods. Mo hits Lam right on the chin, just hard enough to knock him out and leave a visible bruise. Mo, with his Glock stuck in the back of the fake Charlie Long, walks out the side door of the district police station to the waiting Jaguar driven by Cookie.

Mo pushes the fake Charlie Long into the backseat while he gets in the front beside Cookie. Cookie stomps on the gas pedal like she's trying to kill an escaped tarantula that found its way into her Jag. She swerves around corners just like every other crazy driver on the island. She looks at Mo, "Who the fuck is that?"

Mo: "Charlie Long…"

Cookie: "That's not Charlie Long!"

Mo: "He says he's Charlie Long."

Cookie: "Not our Charlie Long…"

Mo: "I know…" Mo turns in his seat, "Who the hell are you?" The fake Charlie Long looks puzzled.

Mo: "Ask him, who he is?"

Cookie looks in the rearview mirror as she takes another corner way too fast: "*Nǐ jiào shénme míngzì?*"

The fake Charlie Long smiles, "*Nǐ yào wǒ shì shéi?*"

Mo: "What did he say?"

Cookie: "He asked, who do want him to be?"

Mo turns in his seat and looks the fake Charlie Long in the eye. The guy smiles a big broad smile exhibiting his prized gold tooth. Mo raises his gun and shoots him in the head. "Now it doesn't matter who the fuck he is."

Cookie: "Are you going to help clean that up? This car's a renter." Cookie turns the wheel hard onto an alley heading for a warehouse where they will leave the car for their associates to handle while Mo gets on a plane back to the States and Cookie heads back to London.  "Well... at least we eliminated one Charlie Long."

Mo: "Yeah, the wrong Charlie-fucking-Long."

**Death For Dessert**

## 21
## Death for Dessert
## A Montoya Family Dinner

It's been said that dinnertime is family time; time for Mom, Dad, the kids, and maybe even Uncle Sam to gather around and tell each other about their day. It's like Christmas, a time for good food, humorous stories, and a feeling of wellbeing that makes everyone imagine all is right with the world. It's bullshit of course. The truth is dinnertime, fueled by kicking back a dozen after work beers, or maybe even something stronger if you're in a higher tax bracket, is time for taking out your frustrations.

It starts with bitching about all the dumb-asses you had to put up with during the day and ends with accusations over some long half-forgotten incident that your spouse has completely forgotten about. Dinner starts with grace and ends with throwing dishes, crying kids, and sleeping on the couch. Dinnertime is like negotiating with North Korea. You just know, sooner or later, the crazy son-of-a-bitch sitting opposite will fire off a missile. Okay... maybe that's a bit cynical, but really, dinnertime ain't no fucking Hallmark card, and in the case of the Montoyas, it's downright uncivil war.

Tonight is party time at the Montoya hacienda. Guests have gathered from near and far, and the kitchen has been told to do it up right. Tonight

Alejandro Montoya intends to cleanup loose ends, to make a statement so that everybody including, his daughter, the Chinese, and Section Six understand nothing happens without him and his chili. By the time dessert is served Montoya intends to have eliminated his enemies and taken control of the Southern California cocaine market.

With the disappearance of Charlie Long, Montoya figures he's perfectly positioned to take over what's left of the Wan Chai operation. He may not be Chinese or speak the tongue, but money is the universal language, and just as importantly, he controls the chili. He figures it shouldn't be too hard to convince the remaining Wan Chai and what's left of the *Jiangshi* motorcycle gang to play along. And once he does, the Hong Mian and Benson Yeung will be toast. The Englishman and his peanut butter operation can either go along or not. There are plenty of other options: desperate companies looking to expand their product line with the most profitable consumable on the market.

The dinner guests include William Stone, the money launderer representing the Hong Mian and Section Six; Victor Wong, Charlie Long's State-side right-hand man; Sonya Montoya, Alejandro's fed-up punching bag daughter; some blonde piece-of-ass (Jesse) that Sonya says is an old school buddy; the thug that paid Margarita a visit at the pink gallery; and a surprise guest that

Alejandro intends to spring on the group. Tension is served as an appetizer.

The Montoya dining room is an elaborate affair with a large heavily carved round table able to seat twelve, Each of the current six chairs that surround the table are also hand-carved by a local craftsman and upholstered in red velvet. Heavy matching red velvet drapes keep the sun from penetrating the large picture windows that frame the room. A wide patio door leads to the outside where breakfast is usually served and double doors lead to the hallway and front entrance. The ceiling is vaulted with exposed curved beams and a hideously ornate gold-colored chandelier that adds just the right extraneous ostentatious touch. On the far wall is a large gold mirror that reflects an equally large full-length portrait of Montoya looking every bit the hardworking late nineteenth century *ranchero*: a fictitious representation of a man whose hands were more used to weekly manicures than a day mending fences in the back-forty.

The table is elegantly set with fine china and crystal goblets. Sonya informed her father earlier in the day that Teresa, the cook, had to return home to her village to care for her sick mother, news that prompted Papa Montoya to strike his daughter with a vicious backhand causing a significant welt. Dinner would have to be ordered from Cacaloxuchitl's favorite fast food eatery, the *Palacio Del Pollo De Diego*. Sonya told Diego to

come up with something very special for her father. On seeing the bruise under Sonya's left eye,
Diego understood the importance of his recipe
choice.

Diego's daughter helps her father serve each
course starting with a delicious mixed green sal-
ad. An appropriate white wine from a local vine-
yard is served to quench the guests' thirst. Montoya sits at what one would surmise is the head
of the table despite the fact the table is round.
Sonya sits to her father's left and Jesse sits on his
right just close enough for Alejandro's hand to
occasionally find its way to Jesse's inner thigh.
Stone sits next to Jesse and Victor Wong sits next
to Stone. There are two more seats around the
table that are currently empty.

At one point Jesse drops a piece of lettuce onto
her lap while Montoya's hand is slowly seeking
its target. With one sharp thrust of her fork, Jesse
jabs for the leafy green wanderer, purposely
missing, and instead, finding the back of Alejandro's hand. No one but Stone reacts to the painful
yelp that comes out of Montoya's mouth. Stone
just smiles, silently acknowledging that Jesse is
as good with a fork as she is with a knife. Alejandro excuses himself to seek some alcohol and a
bandage. When he returns dinner nervously continues until everyone finishes their salads.

Montoya's thug from the art gallery enters the
dining room and whispers something in Alejan-

dro's ear. The thug hands Alejandro an envelope. Alejandro speaks to his man, "Yes, yes, bring her in, we've been waiting for her. She's just in time for the main course."

The surprise guest has arrived. The thug leaves the room and without much fanfare flings Margarita Cervantes into the dining room almost causing her to fall. Stone is furious, he starts to make a move but Jesse grabs his arm digging her nails deep into his forearm, Stone sinks back into his seat.

Montoya: "My men went to visit Mr. Stone's little art gallery in Palermo and look what they brought back, the lovely Margarita Cervantes, Mr. Stone's pretty assistant. And all I expected was a painting, but the lovely Margarita is certainly as pretty as a picture."

Jesse can sense Stone's temper starting to boil over. She reaches for Stone's hand, squeezing it gently, signaling him to calm down, she's got his back. Stone relaxes. Margarita takes her chair beside Victor Wong with the thug taking the remaining seat.

Stone looks at Margarita, "Are you all right?" Margarita nods.

Montoya: "Of course she's all right. I'm a civilized man. I thought you'd be happy to see your little playmate."

Jesse drops her right hand, so it hangs down just above her boot. She feels for her pearl-handled switchblade. It wouldn't take much; one quick movement and she could easily find his carotid artery. Sonya senses what Jesse is thinking and surreptitiously shakes her head.

Montoya: "Let's see what's inside this envelope. It must be important or Eduardo wouldn't have left it here for me to look at now." Alejandro removes a photograph from the envelope. It's the photo of Jesse on Medicine Hat that sat on Stone's desk.  "Now look at this," he holds up the photo so everyone can see it, "it's a picture of my daughter's old school pal on a horse all dressed up like a real jockey."

Montoya turns to Jesse: "Tell me my dear, is this one of those fancy special effects pictures where you get dressed up like a fireman or policeman with a painted background like you're a *puto héroe?*"

Jesse: "Yeah… fucking cool special effects. It was either a jockey or triad ninja. I figured the horse shit made more sense."

Montoya: "It almost looks real, but I can spot a fake from a mile away. I wonder where Eduardo found this little gem of a photo. I'll have to ask him after dinner."

Diego and his daughter enter with trays loaded with dishes of Diego's new recipe of Montoya Sweet Chili Chicken with Cashews.  Each plate is piled high with chicken. The top piece on each plate displays a decorative flag with one of the guests' names on it. Montoya smiles at Diego's attention to detail. He claps his hands together, "*Bravo mi amigo! Bravo!*"

Montoya is the first to try his chicken, he nods his head in appreciation, "Diego my friend, you have outdone yourself. This delicious new recipe seems to have some unique secret ingredient. What's in it?" Montoya shovels more of the chicken and chili into his mouth.

Diego: "Thank you *Señor* Montoya. Please every-one, enjoy." Everyone starts to eat.

Montoya: "You must tell me the secret ingredient," as he downs more of the chili and chicken. Diego begins a long explanation of how he prepared the new dish. As Diego's complicat-ed description drags on, Montoya's heart begins to race.

Diego: "Oh yes, I should mention, for *Señor* Mon-toya's dinner I used a special cassava that is high in cyanogenic glucosides that is known to cause Konzo, or cyanide poisoning." Everyone stops eating. Sweat starts to bead under Montoya's nose and on his forehead.

Diego: "I also used raw cashews for *Señor* Montoya's dinner. Real raw cashews that have not been steamed like the ones you buy in the store. Raw cashews contain urushiol, the same chemical you find in poison ivy." Montoya's throat starts to go numb.

Diego: "And oh yes, I almost forgot. I sprinkled a generous helping of cocaine on *Señor* Montoya's dinner." Diego looks around the table. Everyone around the table, except Sonya, is wide-eyed, feeling their throats trying to tell if they too have been poisoned. "One way or another, one of those ingredients will kill the bastard." Montoya reaches for his stomach and collapses into what's left of the sweet chili chicken and cashews.

Eduardo reaches for his cell phone and calls for an ambulance. Victor Wong abruptly stands knocking his heavily carved red velvet ornate dining room chair backwards onto the floor. He reaches for his gun tucked into the small of his back, swinging it around in the direction of Diego, but Diego's daughter hits him in the back of the head with the silver tray she used to carry in the chicken. Wong is stunned for a second, giving Jesse just enough time to retrieve her pearl-handled blade, firing it across the table finding its mark in Victor Wong's throat. He grabs for the knife with his free hand but Stone is on his feet. He delivers a vicious karate below just under Wong's nose. Despite what you've heard or seen in the movies, this does not drive the nose into the brain since the nose is made-up of malleable cartilage that cannot penetrate the skull, something Stone who was trained by Section Six specialists, knows well. Wong falls backwards hitting his head on the tile floor jarring his gun free.

Stone bends down retrieves the gun and fires one shot into Wong's chest and another into Wong's forehead. Meanwhile Eduardo has Margarita in an arm-lock around her chest with a gun to her head as he starts backing up to the two large doors that lead to the hallway and the front door.

Eduardo: "*¡Acércate y yo la mataré!*" No translation is necessary, the anger, the gun, and the look on Margarita's face says it all. Eduardo continues to back up close to the dining room's double doors. Margarita is scared, but her voice is clear and steady, "Shoot the bastard! William… for god's sake shoot the *hijo de puta*."

The double doors fly open as two paramedics enter the room. The doors hit Eduardo in the back knocking him forward forcing him to loosen his grip on Margarita, allowing her to duck free. She elbows him in the groin before she dives for cover. Stone fires. POP! POP! POP!

Eduardo staggers backwards through the open double doors as each slug enters Eduardo's chest. The paramedics hit the floor along with everyone else. Stone walks slowly towards Eduardo and stands over him as he watches him bleed. Margarita appears to his left. Jesse appears on his right. All three watch Eduardo as he silently pleads for merci.

Margarita: "*Hijo de puta.*"

Jesse: "Yeah... finish the motherfucker!"

Sonya appears beside Jesse: "Do it!" Stone fires the *coup de grâce*.

The paramedics have the semi-conscious Montoya onto his feet and together drag him out to the waiting ambulance. Diego and his daughter approach.

Diego: "Are you going to let them take him to the hospital?"

Sonya: "Don't worry, they're not going to the hospital." She turns to Margarita, "My dear... didn't you recognize your parents?"

Juan Pedro Cervantes and his wife Maria dressed like paramedics load Montoya into the back of an ambulance. Juan Pedro takes the wheel while his wife sits in the back watching Montoya moan. She holds a hypodermic needle filled with enough morphine to kill a horse. She injects Montoya. Alejandro Montoya has been retired.

**Stone Cold**

# 22
## Stone Cold

**Three Months Later**

The residue of the Wan Chai and *Jiangshi* are keeping a low profile. They haven't recovered to the point where they are capable of interfering in the new working alliance of Sonya Montoya, William Stone, and Benson Yeung. Sonja has replaced her volatile father and is running her end of the business in a thoughtful, reliable manner. Stone and Jesse now live together in the penthouse of a newly finished luxury condo, part of the ever-expanding Hancock Entertainment Complex. Stone continues his money-laundering operation from the newly opened *La Galeria de Rosa*, LA, leaving Margarita Cervantes in charge of the Palermo gallery.

Stone maintains his absentee ownership position in the Murphy Peanut Butter Company, leaving day-to-day operations in the capable hands of Zack Wei and Genghis Lee. The chaos created by Charlie Long and his associates is gone, but Long is out there somewhere just waiting for his opportunity to strike.

The Imperial Palace Hotel is located on Jung Jing Road between Gin Ling Way and Lei Mein Way in the heart of LA's bustling Chinatown. The Palace is a commercial hotel frequented by traveling salesmen in need of a clean, respectable place to stay with amenities designed to serve the needs of businessmen living out of their suitcases. The food is passable and the service tolerable, but the clincher is the barbershop. It offers hot towel shaves, manicures, and expert shoe shines. It isn't what Charlie Long is accustomed to, but then gangsters on the run with a price on their heads from rival criminal groups can't be choosey.

Fancy, it isn't, but the slightly tacky, imitation Chinese architecture, decoration and kitsch serve to provide a cheap and convenient hiding place. Charlie Long blends in perfectly amongst the dominating Chinese population of the area. It is a place where Charlie Long can hide in plain sight.

The cardinal rule of professional gangsters is never form a pattern of behavior, but successful people get lazy and arrogant; they figure they are untouchable. Every morning at ten in the morning Richard Xiao enters the Imperial Palace Barbershop and Shoeshine Parlor. He takes a seat in one of the black leather barber chairs and reads the LA Times until Freddie, the barber, finishes working on his current customer.

While waiting, one of the interchangeable manicure girls in tight white slacks and crisp white shirts open to reveal just enough cleavage to slow down even the busiest businessman prepares a hot towel. When the towel is ready, the manicure girl drops the barber chair back in the reclining position and applies the towel. Each of the customer's hands are placed in separate bowls of warm water to soak in order to soften the cuticles for manipulation.

It is a self-indulgent exercise in pampering that seems somehow out of character for someone who has spent his entire life getting his hands dirty, both literally and figuratively.  With Xiao reclined under a hot towel with his hands soaking in warm water, Lenny, the shoeshine guy, rhythmically slaps Xiao's handmade eighteen hundred dollar Berluti loafers with a syncopated flair worthy of a Joe Morello drum solo. Some habits are hard to change.

Charlie Long had to laugh at the Hong Mian's feeble attempt to eliminate him. He had friends and contacts just like Benson Yeung. The price was steep, but ultimately money talks. As far as the Hong Kong police where concerned Charlie Long was killed by a gunshot to the head by a co-conspirator during his failed escape. The poor slob who took Charlie's place in jail was ultimately found floating beside one of the docked Hong Kong-Kowloon ferries, causing some tourists to lose their continental breakfasts. Charlie Long was gone forever.

The passport of the man who enters the Imperial Palace Barbour Shop and Shoeshine Parlor every morning at ten in the morning says its owner is Richard Xiao, Import Export entrepreneur, a man who has a remarkable resemblance to the not so dead Charlie Long, but then, context is everything when it comes to recollection and memory.

The woman at the head of the line giving the poor underpaid store cashier a hard time about the company's failure to price match is the same woman you see every week at the bank who cashes your paycheck. Context... when you remove people from their normal environment they disappear into the farthest reaches of your subconscious: out of context, out of mind. The brain is a marvelous instrument, able to solve the most complex of puzzles, but re-frame the pieces in a random context, and the mind says, "fuck it," who cares. It is a mistaken reliance on this mental flaw that sets the scene for what is about to happen.

Richard Xiao enters the Imperial Palace Barbour Shop and Shoeshine Parlor right on schedule. Freddie, the barber, works on a well-dressed customer at the far end of the shop. The customer's head is hidden behind the morning newspaper. Another customer sits reclined in one of the black leather barber chairs with a hot towel wrapped around his face. Xiao waves to Freddie who acknowledges his arrival.

Freddie: "Be with you in a few minutes Mr. Xiao, as soon as I finish here."

Xiao spots a new manicure girl preparing a hot towel in one of the sinks. The woman has jet-black hair, a narrow waist, and a great ass. Xiao takes a seat in the empty third barber chair.

Xiao: "New girl Freddie?"

Freddie: "Just a temp till Maggie gets back, but she gives a killer shave."

Xiao: "I hope she's as good as she looks."

The woman turns around. It's Jesse in a jet-black wig, over-the-top makeup, and a shirt that has trouble containing her breasts. She's chewing gum, hips thrust to one side, with a hand on her narrow waist. Xiao or Long if you prefer has seen Jesse around although they've never been formally introduced. She looks familiar, but out of context with the black wig and overtly sexy outfit, he can't place her.

Jesse: "Okay cowboy you ready for a killer shave?"

Before Xiao can respond Jesse grabs the lever on the barber chair dropping the back into a reclining position. Xiao flops backward like a lake trout that just realizes the seemly tasty insect he just bit isn't a tasty insect at all. Xiao is about to object but Jesse leans hard over him pressing her nearly exposed breast into his body.

Jesse: "Relax baby, Mama's gonna give you something special."

Xiao tries to relax but before he knows it, Jesse slaps a steaming hot towel over his face. Xiao utters something that sound a lot like "what the fuck are you doing?" but the towel muffles most of what he says. He starts to get up but can't because the chair has been put in an almost horizontal position. He tries to reach for the towel to remove it but he feels one large male hand grab his wrist and yank it back onto the arm of the chair. He feels one of those black plastic zip-ties tighten around his wrist. A more delicate female hand grabs his other wrist, but delicate or not, it's fucking strong; strong enough to make a thousand pound thoroughbred do what she wants. Another zip-tie secures his second wrist. The towel is removed. His face is beet red.

Jesse stands to one side of Xiao's barber chair with her hands on her hips. The man in the next chair who had a hot towel covering his face is zip-tying Xiao's ankles to the footrest. It's Stone. Jesse shoves a corner of the hot towel in Xiao's mouth stifling any objection or cry for help.

Xiao looks around. The man sitting in the far chair is still there, still reading the morning edition of the LA Times. Freddie is standing in front of the locked entrance wearing his coat and hat. He's pulled down all the window shades blocking any view from the outside. He's placed a 'Closed For The Day' sign on the front door.

Freddie: "You'll clean up when you're finished."

The man reading the newspaper puts it down and gets up out of the chair. He folds the newspaper carefully and places it on a table beside some old editions of *Sport's Illustrated* and *Playboy*. The man is Mo Fields. He approaches Freddie and hands him a thick envelope.

Mo: "As promised… and not to worry, the place will be spick-and-span when you open in the morning."

Freddie leaves through the back door. Mo approaches Xiao's chair. He stands at the foot of the chair with Jesse on one side and Stone on the other. Xiao is desperately flinging his head from side to side incoherently jabbering away as best he can with the still hot towel rammed into his mouth.  He sees Stone, and that brings everything into view. The girl must be that ex jockey bitch, and the other guy… shit… it's Mee Field's husband.

Mo undoes the button on his custom Zegna suit jacket revealing the black leather shoulder holster and its Glock semi-automatic occupant. He reaches into the inside pocket of his jacket and retrieves his iPhone. He dials.

Mo: "Hi Cookie… when did you get into town? Good… I'm glad you had a safe flight. So, a couple of friends and I are having a going-away party for a fellow… and well… you know how parties can get. Could be messy. Think your cleaner can do us a solid? That's great, I'll text you the address. So why don't you join us for a little after-party dinner tonight. Sounds good. See you tonight."

Mo Fields sighs, a deep sad sigh. He stares Charlie Long in the eye for a very long minute. He pulls out his Glock, takes a suppressor out of his jacket pocket, and screws it into the end of the gun. Every movement is deliberate. This is one execution he wants to savor. He fires three times. The muffled pops are drowned out by the outside traffic noise. Mo continues to stare at the lifeless remains of Charlie Long. Jesse takes a hold of his hand and squeezes.

Mo: "He shouldn't have killed Mee. He shouldn't have killed my wife."

**Loose Ends**

**23**
**Epilogue**
**Loose Ends**

Genghis Lee and William Stone sit on a plaza bench in Passaje Santa Rosa, Lima, Peru. The plaza is a sea of colonial architecture dressed in various shades of yellow ranging from lemon to khaki. The plaza is lined with two facing rows of brightly colored buildings with curved archways that protect the entrances to the various shops from the midday sun. Lee pays special attention to the carved entrance of the *Tiempos Altos* restaurant.

Stone: "People here like yellow."

Lee: "I guess, anything that brightens this shit-hole would help."

Stone: "Why are we here?"

Lee: "The DEA with the co-operation of the Colombian government has been destroying the coca fields in Colombia for years. It's finally having an impact.  Production has moved back to Peru where it used to be before President Fujimori started shooting down the planes moving the coca to the Colombian labs."

Stone: "What's changed?"

Lee: "Fujimori's in jail, he caught a bad case of presidential corruption."

Stone: "This seems like Sonya's problem not ours."

Lee: "Yes and no. We still have a Wan Chai loose end that's found its way to the land of Machu Picchu and Puma Punku."

Lee draws Stone's attention to the four men leaving the *Tiempo Altos.* Two of the men are obviously bodyguards. They wear casual clothes with windbreakers that only occasionally hide the firearms dangling from their shoulder holsters. The presumed boss wears an expensive lightweight leather jacket, dress slacks, and what looks like expensive Italian loafers. The fourth man is Tommy The King Kong.

Lee: "You just can't kill that fucker."

Stone: "Who's the big shot?"

Lee: "They call him *El Astronauta*, his real name is Marco Antonio Suarez.

Stone: "The Astronaut? What's up with that?"

Lee gets up and motions Stone to follow. They watch as the four men get into a black SUV and ride off. "Some people think those Nasca lines were created for aliens. One of them looks like an astronaut. They say the guy is a freak, like he's an alien or something. So locals call him *El Astronauta*. Everybody's got to have a fucking nickname."

Stone: "I don't."

Lee looks at Stone and smiles. "You sure about that? Come on, let's eat." They start walking toward the *Tiempo Altos*.

Stone: "So what now?"

Lee: "War my friend… fucking war."

**The End**

# Author Biography

Jerry Bader is Senior Partner at MRPwebmedia.com, a media production company that specializes in Web video, audio, music, and sound design. Mr. Bader has written and produced dozens of video commercials for clients. Writing scripts and novels is a natural extension that grew out of the experience of creating attention-grabbing mini movies that focus on the core emotional motivator.

Over the years Mr. Bader has written over a hundred articles on marketing, and he's self-published marketing e-books, hybrid graphic novels, biographies, and a series of children's books. The Neo Noir Hybrid Graphic Novels are story concepts developed with the goal of having them turned into television series or feature films. There are currently ten screenplays, five of which have been self-published as hybrid graphic novels: *The Method, The Comeuppance, The Coffin Corner, Grist For The Mill* and *The Black Crane.*

He's also written *The Fixer* published by Rebel Seed Entertainment. It has consistently been in the top ten percent in several Amazon categories. *The Fixer* is based on the true-life story of a colorful horse racing character. The follow-up to *The Fixer* is the new book *Beating The System* that continues the story of the horse racing legend.

Mr. Bader has also written *Organized Crime Queens, The Secret World of Female Gangsters, What's Your Poison? How Cocktails Got Their Names, Cowboys, Lawmen, and Outlaws, The Outlaw Rider, Dead End, Palermo, Stone Cold, and the soon to be released: The Aussie Switch,* and *Ballet Of Bullets.*

Mr. Bader has also written a series of children's books, ZaZa Books For Kids, that currently includes, *Two Dragons Named Shoe, The Town That Didn't Speak, The Criminal McBride, The Bad Puppeteer, Mr. Bumbershoot, The Umbrella Man, The Ninth Inning,* and *14 Ridiculous Tales of Sage Silliness.*

# The Outlaw Rider

If you're not prepared to cheat, you're not prepared
to win.

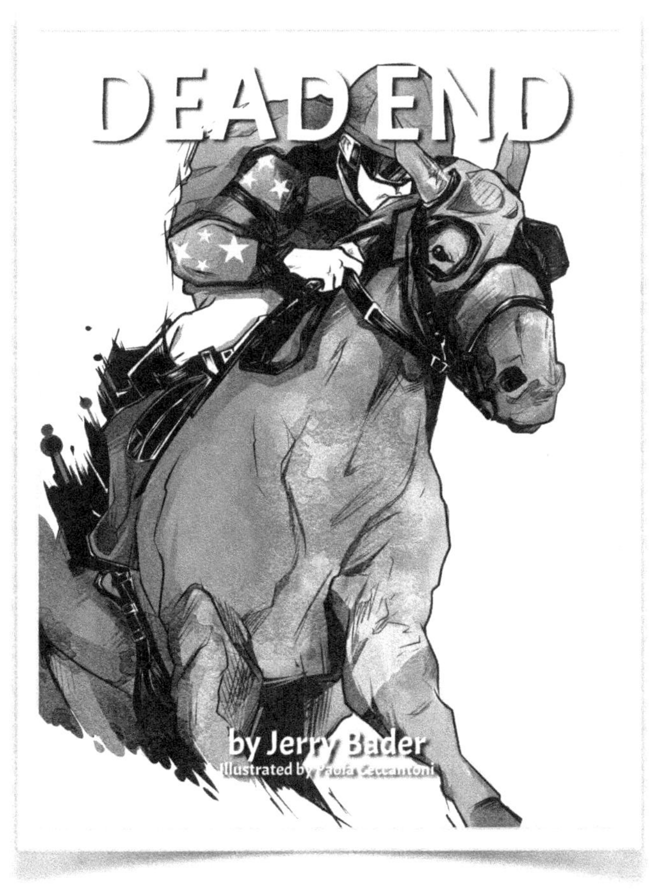


# Dead End

There Are No Good Guys

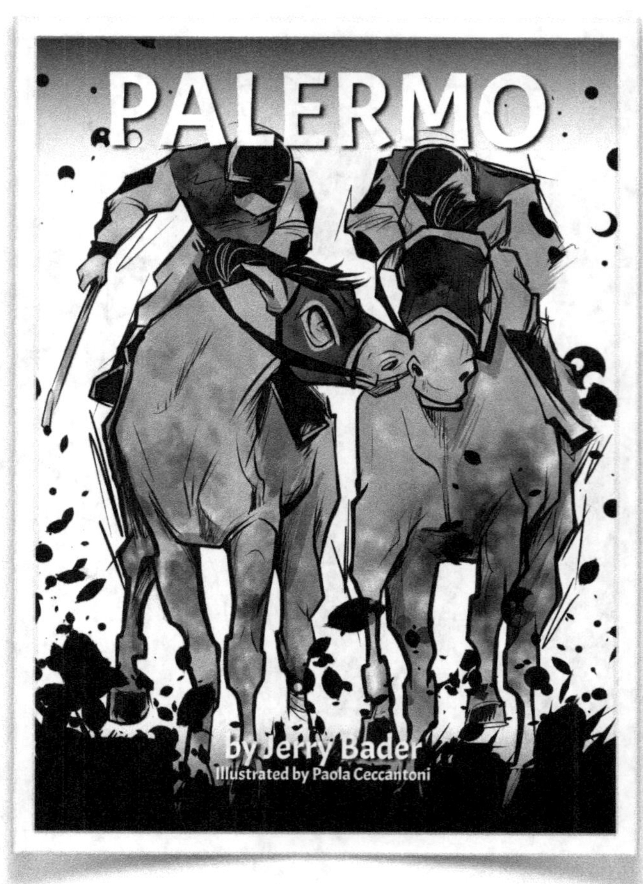


# Palermo

A Place To Die

# Beating The System

Beat the odds. Beat the system, Survive!

# NOIR I

The Gold Cricket, The Bastard,

Cine City, and Killer Jazz

# NOIR II

Cult, The Red Emperor, The Redhead Rip-Off,
and The Incident Report

# Organized Crime Queens

The Secret World of Female Gangsters

# Cowboys, Lawmen, and Outlaws

The Myth of The American Psyche